THE PAL
Ro

MW00713311

The Palouse Horse, a historical fiction, focused on the story of a Nez Perce Indian, Matthew, his ancestors and their spotted horses. In Book II, Rollie's Story, the saga continues with Matthew's friend, cowboy Rollie Burroughs, his pioneer family, Indian friends, various people and coworkers, as well as the personable animals, in his life.

(Borein)

By
Susan Shuttleworth

Susan Shuttleworth Holland
Quincy, Fl.
2006

Copyright © 2006
Susan Holland

All rights reserved. No part of this book may be reproduced in any form, except for the inclusion of brief quotations in a review, without permission in writing from the author or publisher.

Library of Congress Card Number: 1-304-138

ISBN 0-9753462-1-0

Printed in the U.S.A. by
Morris Publishing
3212 East Highway 30
Kearney, NE 68847
1-800-650-7888

ACKNOWLEDGMENTS

Joe Libertucci, my dearest friend, has been invaluable with support, advice and technical assistance. He has been with me every step during the creation and development of The Palouse Horse II, Rollie's Story. This book is dedicated to him with my love and appreciation.

A special thank you to Mr. Peter Chapin for his assistance and encouragement.

Although the book is a historical fiction, many of the stories told by Rollie's elderly aunt are loosely based on some of our own Missouri family stories. The anecdotes have been modified to fit the characters in the book and their own circumstances. My sister, Barbara Dempsey deserves special credit for her assistance and input. Many of our family stories would have died without her knowledge and preservation of them.

One anecdote regarding the Indian in the kitchen (Chapter Six) was loosely based on an incident provided by Ada Teague, a member of an Indian River County, Florida pioneer family. The girl was one of the family's children and the Indian was a local Seminole.

Last but not least, a number of the other characters in the book are based on interesting Indian River County, Florida people that I know and admire…. with their permission of course. To them, I say "Thank you for playing a part in Rollie's Story."

.

~ William F. Shuttleworth ~
&
Dr. Friel
Standardbred

St. Louis, Missouri - 1904

Red River
aka Smokey Joe
Mustang

TABLE OF CONTENTS

THE PALOUSE HORSE II
Rollie's Story
By Susan Shuttleworth

FOREWORD

The Palouse River flows through the Columbia Basin in northwestern Idaho. Early white settlers to the area observed the local Indians with unusually spotted horses that they raised. They began referring to the spotted horses as Palouse or Palousey horse. The name evolved with a number of variations until Appaloosa began the official name agreed upon by The Appaloosa Club in 1938.

The Palouse Horse (2004)
(Excerpt from the Foreword)

Those who have read The Palouse Horse will remember Matthew, the Nez Perce Indian, and Rollie Burroughs, foreman of the Clyatt's ranch. The story concentrated on Matthew and his passion to find and restore his family's prized herd of Palouse horses that had been lost during the Indian Wars.

The Palouse Horse II, Rollie's Story, concentrates on cowboy Rollie Burroughs. It moves back in time to tell of Rollie's Missouri ancestors, his childhood and how he was molded into the man that he has now become.

From there, Rollie and Matthew.......well, we will just have to wait and see.

(Borein)

1   *THE AWAKENING*

The old steam locomotive hissed by the station platform and slowed to a stop with the passenger cars in position to load. By the time they took on water and coal it would be another hour before departure time. Rollie Burroughs, the tough, weathered cowboy, watched the passengers unload to stretch and eat before resuming the tedious journey back east and to a gentler civilization. Barely thirty-five years had passed since the last of the Indian Wars and Idaho was still a little rough around the edges in spite of the rapid growth of settlements. Well into the second decade of a new century, the local people were unsure if they really wanted so many newcomers here.

Freddy, the stationmaster, greeted the passengers as they stepped down to the rough planked, wooden platform and directed them to a rest area within the green and white station house. He also pointed out the local café halfway down the dusty main street and to Strube's Mercantile just across the way. The café offered a limited choice of traditional hot meals, while the Strube's carried fresh fruits and vegetables as well as Mrs. Strube's home baked German delicacies. Freddy never mentioned Miz Suzy Jane's tavern just beyond the café, but regular travelers knew food was occasionally offered there with a drink.

Harold and Augusta Jennings, retired missionaries, waited on the platform to board this train east with their two-year-old grandson, Daniel. They were adamant about never returning. No one could guess how their friend, Rollie, was suffering as he stood there to see them off. His wide brimmed Stetson hat shaded sad blue eyes as he struggled to keep the feelings to himself as best he could.

Little Daniel's mother, Helen Jennings, died several days after his birth. The child's father was Matthew, a Nez

Perce Indian, who had grown up with Helen and attended the Indian school where Mrs. Jennings taught. Helen and Matthew loved each other from childhood but sadly for Rollie, he had loved her too. In the end she chose Matthew and ran from her disapproving parents to join the Indians in the high country.

Going back to that time, Rollie felt humiliation for he often bragged to everyone about how he would win her over. One of his greatest pleasures in life had been baiting Matthew at every turn, but the Indian would never give him the satisfaction of fighting back. Then, one day Rollie discovered who Helen's secret love really was and his attack gave Matthew no choice but to fight. Lighter by at least 50 pounds than the big cowboy, Matthew was faster and more agile. Aided by a latent resentment of Rollie's constant torment, the little man beat him handily, then gathered his belongings and left for the mountain home.

In time they all made their peace and life went on. That is, until the day that Matthew carried Helen and their newborn son to the doctor's home in town. When she died there Matthew fled, leaving the baby behind. He never returned and Helen's parents were left to bury their daughter and raise the baby. Most of the town's people did not understand and were unforgiving. But Rollie sympathized to the point that the baby was a reminder of the love that Mathew had lost. He hoped that a day would come when Matthew could love the boy for himself and come back to claim him. In the meantime Rollie was determined to be the substitute dad. He rationalized that by caring for her son, he could hold on to Helen a little longer.

Attending church every Sunday was the biggest sacrifice anyone could ask of Rollie Burroughs. But, if that's what it takes to be accepted by these people, then that's what I will do, he reasoned. Fellow cowboy Purdy Roxlo teased him mercilessly, but Junior Pelly lectured that it was about time that Rollie concerned himself with salvation. Neither caught on that being accepted by the Jennings family in order to see the baby was his only motivation. It didn't take long before there was no pretense to the dad ruse, for that is what he began to feel. The Jennings complained from time to time about being too old for such responsibility and that gave Rollie even more latitude to spend time with the boy. Soon he even took him on short outings to the ranch, where he worked and they spent time looking at the cows and horses. Safely enveloped in Rollie's strong right arm, the tiny little boy sat in front of him in the saddle during their excursions. Ranch owners Sophia and Delmar Clyatt grew to love the little boy also.

Then came the bitter day when the Jennings announced their decision to move back East, taking the boy with them -- never to return. Hearing those words hit Rollie like a kick in the gut.

Dear God, he thought, it's like someone has died again. How am I going to make it through this? For a moment he stood frozen in place and stared at them with widened eyes and gaping mouth. Without a word, he wheeled about and bolted from the house. Running to the livery stable two streets over, he arrived out of breath and red faced. His big Palouse horse was saddled and out the door before the stable master even knew they were gone. The horse was young and strong. Rollie had accepted him reluctantly as a gift from Matthew in better days. A sorrel roan gelding, with only a hint of the typical Palouse horse coloring, he only had one white foot. The color of a horse's feet and legs had always been an obsession with the cowboy and this particular one met his requirements that way.

"Come on boy, don't let me down," he urged, and they galloped toward the darkening hills. Throughout the night they walked and ran, then walked and ran again until by early morning, the wet, exhausted horse trotted into the stable yard on Matthew's mountain ranch. Rollie dismounted in front of Matthew.

Politely and calmly Matthew endured these visits from his angry, exasperated friend many times before, then both went on about their business again. This time, however, his tirade was fueled by panic and anguish.

"It's them Jennings people!" Rollie bellowed as he stalked back and forth... "They're takin Daniel back east tomorrow an not comin back. They wasn't even gonna tell ya. For Christ's sake! Will ya listen to me?"

Matthew's seemed disinterest exasperated Rollie to the point of exploding. His beefy fist slammed into Matthew's face, sending him flying backward to the ground. Rollie pinned the Indian with a boot on his chest. Matthew lay bloody and silent to the rest of Rollie's tirade. In a final act of frustration, Rollie drew back his heavy boot and kicked Matthew's ribs with all his might.

Mounting his weary horse the beleaguered cowboy began a long, lonely ride back down the mountain to the little town and the sorrows that faced him in the morning.

With a broken, bloodied nose and cracked ribs, Matthew retreated to the dark, quiet hayloft where he spent a good part of the day recovering. His mind started to reminisce a childhood with his own parents and how it was to grow up with their love and guidance. His father, Two Feathers, instilled the love and drive to protect and preserve their people's Palouse horses. He raised Mathew in the old traditions with ethics and survival skills of the Nez Perce people. Mary, his mother took him to the missionary's school for white man's education. She reasoned that to survive in the white man's world, he needed to learn their ways. It was there that he met his teacher Mrs. Jennings and her young daughter Helen. Helen befriended him and over time, they developed a closeness that grew beyond a childhood friendship. He remembered his love for Helen and the joy of their expected baby. The baby! Like a heavy blanket, guilt and shame rolled over his body until the breath was almost mashed out of him. With a gasp of pain, he sat upright; finally realizing that while he lay here in the hay Daniel was about to be taken away forever.

The train's one-hour rest stop was almost half over. Rollie paced the wooden platform, not even aware of what he did. Water from the elevated wooden tank adjacent to the tracks had been emptied into the locomotive's boilers and workers had filled the coal car to an imposing black, gleaming heap.

"Please don't let me cry," he silently begged an invisible god. As he turned to go back down the platform, Mr. and Mrs.

4

Jennings climbed the stairs at the opposite end. The stationmaster pulled a cart loaded with luggage up a ramp and prepared to load it on the train for them. They were both dressed in formal black traveling clothes: she in the typical long skirted dress with a high collar and cameo pin, and he in a dark suit and white shirt. Augusta Jennings held the little boy's hand. Still in diapers, Daniel wore the typical little boy's white cotton dress -- scalloped sleeves and neck, the skirt descending almost to his ankles, high-top white stockings and black slippers with cross straps. A decorative matching fabric belt hung loosely around his hips. His shortly cropped black hair was still slightly wet and combed upward on the top of his head into a big curl.

"Uncle Rollie," Daniel squealed, holding out his hands for the cowboy to take him. Rollie hustled down the platform, grabbed the boy up and almost crushed him against his huge body.

Suddenly, from atop the distant hill a shrill, wild shriek caused them to start and jerk around. Looking toward the nearest hill he gasped at the sight of a wildly galloping horse with Matthew clinging bareback, hair flying, urging her on faster down the last slope. The sight finally brought the tears to Rollie's eyes and his body sagged weakly with hopeful relief. With the boy still in his arms, he stumbled to a nearby wooden bench and sat down.

Augusta and Harold Jennings stiffened and looked angry. "What is *he* doing here?" Augusta demanded to no one in particular.

"This is not going to be good," countered Harold. Glaring at the approaching horseman, they stood and waited.

The horse slid to a stop at the platform edge, her wet coat sleek and darkened from sweat. Blowing through flared nostrils the mare's fine head drooped with exhaustion. Matthew slid off her back, leaped up onto the platform and approached the little party. He paused in front of Rollie and stared at the little boy in his lap. Daniel's eyes widened in fear, and he buried his face in Rollie's collar. Matthew's face and nose, still bloodied and dirty, were now swollen and purple with bruising. Traces of dirt from the stable yard and Rollie's offending boot still clung to his rumpled shirt. His pants were wet from the horse's sweat and matted with her hair. Wild and disheveled, long black hair flew out in every direction and hung over his face.

Geez, thought Rollie sarcastically, off to a good start old buddy.

On moccasin-clad feet, Mathew proceeded to the Jennings and stood before them. "Daniel is my son," he said simply. "I have come for him."

Reeling, Augusta stepped backward, a pudgy little hand grasped at her chest.

"*No, no, no*," she shrieked. "You're too late. He is ours now and we're leaving. God forgive me, but you should go to hell. Get out of here -- Get out!"

Matthew stood determined in front of the hysterical woman. Harold standing meekly beside his wife kept silent.

Freddy, the stationmaster dropped the cart handle. Eyes wide and hands extended, he pleaded, "Look here folks. Everybody stay calm. I'll get the sheriff and we'll sort this thing out. Jest stay calm - - please."

He jumped off the platform and ran toward the main street as fast as an old man could go. Within minutes, he returned gasping up the platform steps with Sheriff Roy right behind. A tall, lanky man with white hair and a kind face, Sheriff Roy was familiar with all the people involved here today and knew the circumstances well. Soft spoken and articulate, his presence suggested an authority of fairness but no nonsense. The sheriff's very demeanor commanded respect. Taking charge, he walked up behind the glaring Jennings couple, placed a hand on each of their shoulders and leaned forward between them.

"I want you folks to go inside the train station and have a seat. I'll be in directly to talk with you."

Retreating toward the door, their angry eyes never left the Indian's face.

"Okay Matthew," the sheriff said kindly, "let's you and me take a little walk over here and discuss this thing." Matthew

6

stared at the sheriff defiantly. Sheriff Roy walked right up to Matthew and towering over the shorter man he said very deliberately,

"You *will* simmer down and behave or I'm going to throw your ass in jail right now -- then you've got no chance." Roy stared down at the defiant Indian with a steely resolve. "Now git down here with me and let's talk it out real calm-like." After a moment's pause, Matthew nodded slightly and followed the tall man down the platform steps.

Rollie tipped his head back against the station wall and rolled his eyes skyward as the frightened little boy clung to his chest. From the shade of his wide brimmed hat, his blue eyes soon focused on the two men as they talked. He strained to hear their words over noise from the bustling train crew and hissing engine, but to no avail.

Sheriff Roy, arms folded across his chest and head tipped to one side, listened intently to Matthew's side of the story. Savvy to the Indian's discomfort for direct eye contact, he focused beyond Matthew on the steaming locomotive engine behind him. At narrative's end, Roy nodded understanding, gestured for Matthew to stay put and returned to talk with the Jennings.

Rising from her seat in the station, Augusta stepped forward, eager to hear his report. "Okay folks, here's the deal. By all rights, Matthew is the boy's legal father and he has a right to him."

"That's not fair," Augusta shrilled hysterically. "He deserted Daniel and never once came to see him."

"He knows that," countered the Sheriff patiently, and he regrets it more than you kin imagine. He said every time he tried to think of the boy, it brought Helen back. He's still hurtin about her. He's sorry for you, but he wants another chance with his son."

The train whistle shrieked as the stationmaster poked his head around the door. "All 'board, folks," he announced nervously. "The train's gettin ready to pull out."

"Tell the engineer the train stays put until this is resolved," Sheriff Roy said evenly without taking his eyes from Augusta's face.

The stationmaster grimaced, rolled his eyes and retreated back to the conductor who waited outside.

"Sheriff Roy," Augusta began in her sternest schoolteacher's voice, "we're giving this boy a future – he'll have education, manners and a good profession. What can Matthew give him besides those ridiculous spotted horses and a cold home in the mountains?"

"Well, Ma'am, there's more to it than that." Sheriff Roy countered gently. "Matthew and his family can give him a heritage, skills and craftsmanship that no one else can. They will love him. The boy has a right to those things. On the other side, you have more opportunities to offer than most children could ever dream of. You both want the best for this boy." Tipping his head slightly to the side he studied Augusta's face for a sign that his argument had penetrated her mindset. When she still had not responded he reached out to the suffering woman and gently clasped her tiny hands. "Miz Jennings, you have told me yourself, that you felt too old for this much responsibility anymore."

Unable to deny his words, she dropped her eyes in resignation. Tears welled out and streaked down her cheeks.

Harold shuffled to his wife's side. "So is that it than? As I see it, we have a stalemate here."

The train whistled again and the nervous stationmaster started to speak from the doorway, "Sheriff…."

"Dammit, Freddy! If you and that conductor don't back off…. the whole pack of you are going to jail with the Indian if need be. That train sets where it's at until I'm dam good and ready for it to leave! Now, you got that?"

"Yes Sir! Yes Sir! I got it," and he retreated back outside.

From the platform bench where he waited, Rollie watched as the conductor paced nervously up and down the platform. The man continually lifted and studied the big watch attached to a heavy gold chain on his vest. As the clock ticked on, passengers could be seen through the car windows as they fidgeted and complained.

Sheriff Roy finally came outside and approached Rollie. By now, the child was calm and played nearby on the platform.

"Okay Rollie, this is what we've worked out. Besides the Jennings, you are the closest one to the boy. He's comfortable with you. They are willing to share custody with Matthew and give Daniel the benefit of both families in his upbringing. The kid is obviously terrified of his father at this point and that's where you come in."

Rollie's heart pounded, hope and relief washed over him and the tears began to sting his eyes again. He wiped a calloused hand over his face so no one would see.

"If you will take the boy and Matthew out to Clyatt's Ranch"-- the sheriff started and then hesitated. "-- if they will agree to have them there with you" --

"They will!" Rollie interrupted. "I guarantee they will!"

"Okay, get him cleaned up," he nodded at Matthew, who watched from the end of platform. Give them as much time as they need to get acquainted so the boy's not scared anymore, than let them go when you feel the time is right."

"What about them?" Rollie gestured toward the station waiting room where the Jennings waited.

"They're willing to leave now as planned, but will be back next year to visit. Matthew has to agree to share the boy and eventually let him go east for a spell at school. They want the boy college-taught." Roy nodded his head. "And that's good. If Matthew agrees, it's done," concluded the Sheriff.

"Trust me," Rollie puffed. "If he don't agree, than I'm the one who's goin to wind up in your jail tonight." An extended, poking forefinger emphasized his last statement.

Harold and Augusta Jennings composed themselves and said goodbye to their little grandson Daniel. Fighting to hide her anguish, she stooped down and hugged him to her soft bosom. Planting a wet kiss on his cheek, she backed away. "You go with Uncle Rollie now and be a good little boy for

9

Gran," was all she could say in a tremulous voice. Harold intervened with his own hug for the child, then took his wife firmly by the arm and led her toward the train.

Much to Freddy's relief, the conductor was able to move the train out only slightly behind schedule. Matthew received a stern lecture from Sheriff Roy and readily agreed to cooperate with the joint custody terms that had been negotiated. But Rollie, over and beyond all the others, had much to celebrate. Not only was Daniel staying home where he belonged for now, but the coup d'état over Matthew was glorious and full of promise.

2 *TRANSITIONS*

Rollie and the little boy stood in front of the train station watching distant people and animals moving around the town's main street. Sheriff Roy finished his conversation with Matthew and nodded to them as he strode back toward his office. Matthew, following close behind the sheriff turned off toward his boy. Daniel shrieked hysterically, ran terrified to Rollie and clung to his leg.

"Fer god's sake, dumb ass," Rollie spat over the boy's yelling. "Ya look like sumthin rode hard 'n put up wet! The river's over yonder. Why don't ya go make use of it?" He swooped up the boy in one arm, the suitcase with his free hand and stalked up the street toward the livery stable. After settling his account with the stable master, Rollie and Daniel headed back to the main street.

"We're gonna be taking ya out to the ranch purty soon so let's jest walk on down the street here and see if we can't find sumthin to eat first. I got an idea. How bout askin that nice Mrs. Strube to give you a change of britches and then you, me an your Dad'll get some of her good grub. I bet your Dad's hungry as we are."

In times past the Clyatt Ranch's primary business was providing horses for the calvary, with cattle production as a backup. As the long time foreman for Delmar and Sophie Clyatt, Rollie took pride in the quality of the horses produced on the ranch. But as times changed, Delmar shifted over to raising fine Hereford beef cattle. Herding cattle was not Rollie's favorite thing, but he still loved the Clyatts and enjoyed his foreman's status with them.

For Rollie and Matthew, the long ride back to the ranch started on a slow and quiet note. Worn out, both of their horses barely dragged along. Reluctant to approach the little boy again, a cleaner, well fed, Matthew rode silently with his eyes front on the road. Daniel settled into the front of Rollie's deep heavy saddle and leaned back sleeping against the huge man. Almost snoozing himself, Rollie started a little when Matthew suddenly asked,

"Why is my son dressed in girl's clothes?"

"What?"

"Why is my son dressed in girl's clothes?"

"That's what I thought ya said. Simple. He still goes in his drawers. Ya got dress boys an ya got pants boys. He's still a dress boy."

Matthew nodded somberly like this was some great revelation. Obviously, it had bothered him. Another long spell of silence was finally broken when Matthew remarked,

"He thinks you are his father."

"Yeah, he does, an I really wish I was too." he stated sadly. After a moment he glanced over at Matthew and said, "Don't worry bout it, he'll be hanging on ya in no time. I won't meddle tween ya. He jest needed sumbody to be there fer im, that's all."

Relieved, Matthew nodded.

By late afternoon, the ranch buildings appeared in the distance and the weary horses stepped up the pace. Feed and rest were in sight

"We kin fix a little pallet fer Daniel in the bunk house tween our beds," Rollie mused. "That way he kin be near us both in the beginning. I reckon it would be a good idea to send word to yer folks where ye're at so's they take care of things…un let em know their grandson is finally comin home."

The morning when Matthew and Daniel finally left the ranch was the saddest and lowest day that Rollie Boroughs could remember in his life. Pretending to be busy, he spent most of the day hiding out in the barn. In fact he lay in the hayloft staring at the ceiling. He pondered how so much daylight could shine through the cracks, yet when it rained, everything still stayed dry. His mind wandered from life's big mysteries, to little Indian boys and finally to the father of one of them in particular. Jealousy had always played a big part in his relationship with the little Indian man. *He falls in shit and comes out smelling like a rose every time*, Rollie fumed silently to himself. *Here I am, probably over 40 years old, no wife, no young'uns, no home to call my own and don't even know much bout my ma and pa, much less the rest of the family. Hell, I'm not even sure when my birthday is, it's been so long since I thought about it. When I can't pull my weight here anymore, old man Clyatt can toss me out anytime he feels like it an then whut?* He pulled up a sprig of hay and clamped the end firmly between his teeth. Humph! He almost smiled at himself. *At least I do still have all my teeth.*

As the workday drew to a close, Rollie moved stealthily out the back barn door, across the barnyard and into the empty bunkhouse. Purdy Roxlo found him there; lying in his bunk, dirty boots and all, staring morosely at the ceiling. Old Chester, the hound, followed Purdy inside and went to Rollie's bedside. With a cold nose he first poked Rollie's arm and whined. When the man failed to respond the dog laid his head on the arm and stared into Rollie's face with sad brown eyes.

Purdy pulled up a chair and opened his mouth to speak.

"Whatever it is...I don't want ta hear it," Rollie grumbled and flung an arm over his eyes.

"Are ya gonna die over this?" asked Purdy.

"No, I reckon not." he admitted pitifully.

"Than get over it! You're upsetting the dog! B'sides, tomorrow's Saturday and if ya'd get off your ass an help us round here, maybe we could take a ride in ta Miz Suzy Jane's."

Rollie lifted his arm and gave Purdy a weak little smile. "I reckon I could do that," he agreed.

Saturday's at Miz Suzy Jane's place could be raucous. Tonight it was mediocre which was just as well to Rollie, considering his mood. *Anything more than this, I might have to kill somebody* he thought evilly. Miz Suzy Jane, an attractive, but mature woman, loved Purdy. She catered to him with a soft look in her eye and he ate it up. The truth was that he felt a certain warmness toward her as well, but never let things go any further with their relationship than it presently was. Rollie, on the other hand, simply enjoyed the various amenities provided by the establishment and let it go at that. While men drank and joked at the bar, Melvin banged away at the piano, and hostesses plied their trade, the three comrades shared a table and a drink.

Heavily laden with a tray of clean glasses, the young woman walked past them and then used her hip to push the kitchen door open. Rollie looked her way with mild interest, not because she was such a beauty but because she was unfamiliar.

"Who's that?" he asked.

Miz Suzy Jane looked back over her shoulder and replied, "Oh, that's Cecelia Gideon. My new help."

"Well, how's bout callin her over for an introduction. I could use a little of her help," Rollie smirked.

Miz Suzy Jane's blue eyes sparked with a quick temper as she flew into the rowdy cowboy. "Cecelia is not one of the girls. She doesn't want to be and I don't want her to be. She's a trained seamstress, a good cook and all round help. That's how I want to keep her and you can just pass the word. …she's off limits! You understand, that?"

"Yes ma'am! Yes ma'am! I understand." But his eyes never left the woman as she put up the clean glasses, balanced the dirties on her tray and pulled the kitchen door shut behind herself. When his attention turned back to the table, Purdy was giving him a raised eyebrow look that was clearly meant to be a warning. Miz Suzy Jane, usually a pleasant enough, lady-like woman, was subject to a flash temper when crossed. Purdy knew her well enough to know that she meant exactly what she said about the new helper in the kitchen.

Rollie turned his attention back to the glass in his hand and casually asked, "How'd ya find sumbody like her way out here?"

"Actually, it's kind of an interesting story," she answered. "Are either of you familiar with the orphan trains?

14

She came out here on an orphan train when she was just a little thing."

I heared a little bout them." Purdy stated, "Them things ended quite awhile ago though didn't they?"

"No, not really. It's still going on as far as I know."

"What's still goin on? What the hell ya both talking bout." Rollie insisted.

Miz Suzy Jane gave him the evil look and then continued. "Cecelia's folks died in some kind of epidemic back east. Like a lot of other stray kids in the big cities, with no one to look out for them, she was loaded up on the orphan train and shipped west to be adopted by farmers and settlers. I guess some of the kids got pretty good homes but others, like her, didn't have it so good."

Curious, Rollie asked, "What happened to her."

"She told me when the train finally stopped they were in Nebraska. They cleaned the kids up and paraded em around on a wooden platform like animals for auction. Some older couple took her home. The home wasn't too far from their town cause the old lady pretty much supported them as a seamstress. I guess the husband was something of a sot. Cecelia says the lady taught her everything she knew and even spent a little time with what she could of readin and writin. But when she came of age the old man started trying her…. so she ran off. Last year when I passed through the area, I met her selling bread and meat on the train platform. There was just something about her, so I told her my name and where we were if she ever wanted to come out and work. Lo and behold, a couple of weeks ago she just showed up. I don't know how we made it without her before now!" With that last statement, her eyes narrowed slightly in Rollie's direction.

Rollie leaned back in his chair and held his hands up defensively. "Okay, okay. I got the message."

The next Saturday, Miz Sophie asked for one of the hands to drive her to town for provisions. Rollie, who would ordinarily avoid the task, readily volunteered for duty. The first stop was Mr. Strube's Mercantile for fresh fruits and vegetables.

Sophie loved the store because of the variety of their stock and the proprietor's friendly, accommodating manner. Mrs. Strube shared her recipes with the local ladies and told them how to make some of her favorites such as Hasenpfeffer and Dampfnudeln.

After stocking up at the Strubes, Miz Sophie continued her shopping trip up and down the street with visits to the dry goods store and apothecary. While waiting for her, Rollie strolled the streets near Miz Suzy Jane's place in hopes of catching a glimpse of Cecelia Gideon. His hope was rewarded when he looked back at Mr. Strube's in time to see her struggling out the front door loaded with bundles of groceries. He rushed over, tipped his hat and snatched the heaviest bag from her grasp.

"How do ma'am. I'm Rollie Burroughs." She looked at him blankly and he hastened to add, "I seen ya at Miz Suzy Jane's last week and it would be my pleasure to give ya a hand with these bundles." He started to walk away with her bundle and she had no choice but to hasten after him. His brain raced in an effort to make conversation with the woman but nothing appropriate would come. She directed him to the back kitchen door of the saloon, pushed past and up the steps, and then turned to reclaim her package.

A petite, fragile doll, the three-stair step advantage still only brought her to a face-to-face level with the big man. Her complexion was as white and clear as Miz Sophie's best china. Clear blue eyes and dark blonde hair added to her delicate appearance. Although you could not call her beautiful, she was pretty in an innocent, childlike way. His brain momentarily addled, there was nothing for Rollie to do but stand in her presence and stammer. Mistrustful, she began to draw back toward the door, when he blurted in desperation.

"Ma'am, Miz Suzy Jane says yere a seamstress. I wuz wonderin if ya might help me out with some mendin. I got nobody to help me that way an... I could pay ya good." Her face reddened and she nodded in agreement before disappearing into the darkened kitchen.

Excitedly, Rollie snatched off his hat and almost crushed the brim between his two rough hands. "I'll be back to see ya, Miz Cecelia, he called after her. "I'll be bringin my shirts."

Back in the bunkhouse, Purdy Roxlo watched in amazement while Rollie sorted through his meager pile of clothes and began ripping up some of the better pieces. After Rollie confided the mission to his best friend, Purdy warned him about provoking the wrath of Miz Suzy Jane.

"She don't own that girl," Rollie told him, "an I don't think I could stay away even if I wanted. Purdy, I reckon I'm in love again."

Chester's loyalty was rewarded at bedtime with a good ear scratching and a kind word from Rollie. Stretching out on the bunk, a heavy arm across the eyes, Rollie pondered sweet encounters with Cecelia while the dog snored nearby on a braided blue rug. During the night, sweet dreams turned to gray roiling mist, a wiry black mustang galloped through them and a woman cried, lost somewhere in a dark unseen place. Heart pounding, Rollie sat bolt upright, gasping for breath. Clutching at his chest with both hands he struggled free of the covers almost sobbing through deep retching coughs.

This unsettling dream had occurred from time to time all through his life. Since Matthew had taken Daniel away, they came more frequently and gradually evolved in detail. Sometimes, during mundane workdays, his mind wandered to the meaning of it all. Who was the crying woman and why was she crying? I've heard a lot of crying in my time, he thought the morning after the last episode, but never anything like that. It's like a life has ended. Then a slow nod in comprehension… like somebody died again.

3

CECELIA

It took a month before Sophie Clyatt finally figured out why Rollie volunteered every Saturday.

"All this time, I thought you just wanted to help me with the shopping chores and enjoyed the pleasure of my company. Now I find out the real reason. You're trying to court little Cecelia Gideon," she gently teased him as they rode to town.

Several times he began to respond but could do nothing but turn red and move his lips. Regretting her actions, Sophia turned away lest she embarrass him further. When she next glanced over at his face he appeared so distressed that she laid a hand on his arm in reassurance.

"I'm just teasing Rollie," she said. I think Cecelia is a beautiful person and I understand that she is a very talented seamstress." Once again the husky man became flustered and began to stammer something about, "Yeah, she sure can sew."

Sophia slapped a hand across her eyes and forehead. Oh my god, she remembered all the torn shirts that he kept bringing to town. Something was whispered one day about Rollie acting strange and tearing up his clothes. Why can't I just shut up, she chided herself and then quickly changed the subject to Delmar's new horse.

After Sophie's supplies were loaded in the wagon, they parted company. Sophie always liked to visit stores and call on the merchants, while Rollie rushed to knock at the back door of Miz Suzy Jane's establishment. Today Cecelia responded quickly to his knock and for the first time actually seemed pleased to see him there. He looked down at her standing in the doorway and held tightly to his hat with both hands. She looked up into his hopeful, eager face and was not able to suppress a little smile of greeting. For the first time since meeting this big, crude man she was actually able to dismiss the feeling of trepidation that his presence aroused in her. He treated her with respect and courtesy. His adoration was so obvious that it overwhelmed her and she felt amazement that anyone could even care about her. The night before she lay on the hard, narrow little cot that was provided for her off the kitchen and thought about what the morning would bring. The thought of this man once again knocking at her door brought a surprising flush of pleasure. For the first time, she was happy to see him and it showed. Rollie could do nothing but grin down at the tiny woman while hope swelled in his heart.

"It's nice to see you," she said softly. Working the brim of the hat between his strong fingers Rollie could do nothing but continue to grin. He despaired of the words to respond.

"Miz Suzy Jane is away this morning," she finally blurted out. "Would you care to come in and have coffee with me?"

"Yes, Ma'am, I surely would," and he followed her through the door.

Weeks and then months passed with the courtship seemingly progressing at one meeting and then at an impasse the next. Rollie became so distracted that finally even the ever patient Delmar became exasperated and spoke to him about it.

"Dammit, Rollie," he fumed. "If you love this woman so much why don't you just marry her and be done with it? Build a cabin, bring her here and live on the ranch!" Realizing what he had just proposed to the ranch foreman, he slowed down and nodded sagely. "Hmmm, that's really a good idea," he approved his own scheme. Looking back directly into Rollie's sad face, he then spat, "Maybe you wouldn't need to have so many excuses to go running into town and stay here to earn your pay for a change!"

Rollie winced and could not reply. His expression belied great sadness and Delmar could do nothing but soften.

"Okay, okay. Talk to me. If you love each other, what's the problem?"

"Mr. Clyatt, I can't think of nuthin but Cecelia. I asked her to be my wife already but she acts like she's shamed of me

19

or sumthin. Furst off, it wuz slow goin, then she acted like she really wuz excited bout me comin round. Now she don't want nobody to know we're even seein each other and the other day when Miz Suzy Jane started to walk in the kitchen where we wuz talking, she made me hide in the pantry. Miz Suzy Jane don't even know bout me comin round. What kind of way is that to act if ya care bout somebody?"

"Yeah, I agree, that was bad, Rollie. How does she explain herself about that kind of behavior?"

"Miz Suzy Jane is fixin to open a dress and millinery shop," he stated with some sarcasm. She cain't do it without Cecelia, cause she's the seamstress and knows how to make fine lady's dresses….an the hats too. There's no doubt that the two kin make a good dollar from a shop such as that. Cecelia says one day that she loves me an the next time I see her, she's goin on bout that shop. She goes back and forth from hot to cold. I give her my heart an she only sits there tryin to decide if'n she wants it or not. Sometimes, I almost feel she enjoys havin the power. So what more kin I do, Mr. Clyatt?"

"Yep, you do have a real heartbreaker there Rollie. Tell you what I'd do though if I was in your place."

"Whut? Whut?" he asked eagerly.

"I think you're going around too much and making yourself too ready. Why not just stay away for awhile and let her get to missing you."

Rollie's face registered a brief flicker of pain and then acknowledgement that Delmar's plan was logical.

"Next week me an the boys are gonna have the last of the brood mares up ta pasture. If'n ya don't mind, Mr. Clyatt, I'd like to stop off an see Matthew and Daniel fer a day before I come back."

"As long as the work's done first is all I ask Rollie. I hope you find an answer while you're up there."

Shelby, the Clyatt's adolescent son, loved Matthew's parents, old Two Feathers and Mary. Since early childhood, he came to visit and spend time with them on every occasion he could get away from the ranch and his parents. There was no way that Rollie could go to visit that family without him being along too.

Even though Matthew built a modern wood house, barn and various outbuildings on the ranch, his parents could not be lured from their old ways. For more years than anyone could remember they lived in a lodge near the river's edge, just beyond the camas prairie. They finally gave their old home up to be near Matthew on the new up-and-coming mountain ranch. In a stand of cottonwood trees, near the main house, their new lodge was constructed. Cone shaped and covered with grass mats, dirt excavated from the interior floor, was piled around the outside and formed the lower exterior wall. Warm animal skins covered most of the floor with a cleared fire circle in the center. Mary almost always cooked outside though, steaming fish and vegetables on the hot rocks or stews over an open fire in her old iron pots. Just thinking about it made Rollie and Shelby eager to get up that winding mountain road as fast as their horses could be pushed.

The first thing to catch Rollie's eye on arrival was the new wild bunch milling about in a large holding pen. Three of the horses stood out from the rest. Mustangs! Wild Mustangs!

Matthew's father, Two Feathers, hobbled out to welcome the visitors. The old warrior had a difficult time getting around and it saddened them to see him in this state of decline. The visitors swung down from their horses and greeted the old man.

Mary, hearing the voices, peeked around the deerskin lodge flap, then called to little Daniel, "Come quickly, see who is here." Daniel squealed with delight and ran to his Uncle Rollie.

When Matthew rode in later, he found them all gathered around a fire, eating Mary's elk stew and talking the afternoon away.

The next morning found Rollie in a familiar pose by the corral fence. He leaned in with his elbows propped on the mid rail; his forehead propped against the top rail and staring at the horses. He started and looked around when Matthew walked up behind him.

"Still sneakin up on folks ain't ya?"

"It's time you get used to it," Matthew replied with his usual deadpan demeanor. "Seeing you leaning on a fence staring at a certain old buckskin horse is something I've seen a lot of." Rollie winched at the painful dig. Booger, the buckskin that Matthew referred to was moonblind. He had been successfully ridden one fine day by Matthew, but buried Rollie's head in the dirt on his attempt to ride. After his anger and humiliation abated somewhat, Rollie found the horse intriguing and actually grew quite attached to him. Secretly he vowed to ride Booger again one day…. but only when no one was around to watch.

"Hey! Where'd ya find those mustangs?" Rollie quickly changed the subject from the buckskin. "I haven't seen too many of late round here."

"They found us. I just brought these yearlings down from the high pasture yesterday and the wild ones were running with them. I am told some settlers over near the Clearwater Range killed a whole herd – ran them off a ravine onto the rocks. They shot the ones who lived. Guess the mustangs ate too much of their grass…like the buffalo. I think these are what's left of that bunch." Neither Matthew's voice nor his expression belied the sorrow and disgust that he felt in his heart. While he talked, Rollie stared at one small black horse in particular. It caught his eye and he could not look away. The horse had a long, flat body and narrow chest with slim delicate legs. A shaggy forelock topped the fine head and fell across his eyes. Nervous, the little black horse turned to face the man and stared directly back at him. Transfixed, the man could not look away. Something about this horse struck a deep feeling of sadness within him and the feeling was not to be understood.

"Kin I have im?"

Matthew's head snapped around in surprise. "What for? He's no good to you."

"Well, he's no good to you either. I jest want im. He makes me think of something, but I jest don't know what. Did ya ever get a feelin that way, Matthew? I keep trying to remember something and I don't know what it is. That horse there, reminds me."

Matthew nodded assent and the matter was finished.

Around a campfire that evening, Rollie confided his dreams of the roiling gray mist, a woman crying and the black horse. Mary and Two Feathers exchanged a knowing, concerned look. Silence fell over the group as they all stared, deep in thought, at the fire. Finally, the old man spoke.

"The past is calling to you. You will not find peace until you stop to listen."

"You reckon, Two Feathers?" For a moment he stammered before coming up with the words that milled around within his brain. "But how kin I do that? My Ma gave me to my aunt when I was just a little thing. I don't know what happened to my Pa. My aunt tried to be good to me, I reckon, but I wuz jest mad all the time and finally run away."

Mary leaned forward, "Do you know where your aunt is now or if she is still alive?"

"We come from Missouri. If she's still alive, that's where she'd most likely be…still over that old trading post."

The little group chatted the evening away and eventually worn down, rolled into their blankets. They slept around the fire, under a crisp starlit sky. But Rollie's thoughts stayed in the past while he continued to sit silently and stare into the fire.

Morning found the little black mustang tethered snugly between Rollie and Shelby's strong Palouse horses. They dragged him halfway down the mountain kicking and plunging before he finally tired and resigned himself to walk the rest of the way to the Clyatt's ranch. With great relief on their part, he was finally shoved unceremoniously into a corral with the old moonblind buckskin gelding, Booger. Booger raised his head from an ever-present pile of sweet hay, sniffed the air and went back to business, totally uninterested in the newcomer. Delmar was displeased when he saw the wild horse but wisely said nothing about it.

The next Sunday Rollie rode to town, determined to have it out with Cecelia. He wore his best shirt and pants, shined boots and slicked back hair under a fine grey Stetson hat. Cecelia opened the back door to his knock and nervously invited him inside the kitchen.

"I was wondering where you've been Rollie. It's not like you to stay away. Are you alright?" she asked so quickly, the sentences ran together.

Rollie stood in front of the woman. He stared at his boots and fingered the grey hat he held in his hands. Without raising his eyes from the boots, he finally gathered his courage and spoke.

"Cecelia, I stayed away on purpose so ya'd have time to think and maybe ta miss me jest a little. For a while ya seemed so glad ta see me when I'd come round an I began to think about us havin a life together. Then ya start getting cold and it's back an forth till I jest don't know what to think." He raised sad, hopeful eyes and looked her in the face. "Fact is Cecelia, I love ya, an I'm here today to ask fer yer hand in marriage." Her lips parted slightly as if she would speak and he cut her off, talking faster and louder. "I'll work hard ta take good care of ya, I'll build a house, whatever it takes ta make ya happy."

"Rollie...please." She interrupted. "What you say is true and I've been unfair by keeping you off balance. The truth is, I do care for you some, but not enough to be married. You flattered me with all that attention and I was just swept away with it. But I have a chance to work and have a business. I have a chance to be successful and earn money and be respected." The words flooded out in the effort to explain before her resolve failed. "We're going to open the shop and all the fabrics and supplies have been ordered and on the way. Rollie, I'm sorry to hurt you. I just don't want to be tied down now."

Without a word the destroyed man turned and left. The last thing he wanted was for her to see him broken. He walked straight to the train station to purchase a ticket from Freddy, the stationmaster. The next train east was scheduled two days hence and there would be room in the livestock car for his Palouse horse.

"Guess I'll show those folks back in Missouri what a real workin horse looks like," he told Freddy. On the long ride back home he kept hearing Cecelia's words over and over, "I just don't want to be tied down." Well, he thought, that's just great fer you, but how do I get up ever mornin an keep workin my life away with nuthin to make it worthwhile. I jest don't think I kin face another day of it. It was on that ride he resolved to go find his old aunt. Surely, Mr. Clyatt would understand and Purdy and Shelby could look out for Booger and the mustang until he returned.

Rollie's few meager possessions were tied to the back of his saddle in a bedroll. Astride the Palouse horse he rode away from the ranch and toward a train that would take him back to a Missouri past he could barely remember.

One fine sunny morning after he left, Miz Sophie stretched her clothesline from the cottonwood trees that shaded her back yard and began hanging the wet laundry. Every Monday it was the same chore. Build a fire under the big black kettle to heat the water. Scrub the clothes and linens on a scrub board with her own homemade lye soap. The soap was made from cooking grease and the fat from the animals that they occasionally butchered. She stored it in a crock down at the springhouse until enough had accumulated for soap making. When the crock was finally full she dissolved lye into fresh boiling water. Then added the grease and fat and boiled it several more hours until the whole mixture became soapy. She had a special shallow tub where it was then poured to cool and set up. Eventually she cut this into cakes and stored away until laundry day. Her laundry was all rinsed in a second kettle, wrung out as best she could and draped over the line to dry. Today while Sophie labored, her thoughts wandered to how tired she was getting of all this. Maybe it's a sign I'm getting old, she thought. Straightening up, she placed both hands in the small of her back, stretched, then wiped a wisp of hair from her face.

A black speck far down the lane leading up to the ranch caught her eye and she watched a lone horse drawn buggy approaching. Any other time a visitor could be a welcome diversion but not today. I really don't feel up to this today, she thought.

It was a fine little buggy with black leather top and sparkling black spoke wheels. A petite woman in a stylish blue dress and feathered hat drove. Her dark blonde hair was pulled back in a smart upswept do. Wispy curls escaped to frame her delicate face. She pulled up at the picket gate and Miz Sophie went to greet her.

"Hello, Mrs. Clyatt. We've not met before, but I'm Cecelia Gideon."

"How do you do, Miss Gideon? I've heard very nice things about you. Would you like to step down and come in?"

"Thanks all the same ma'am but I'm here to see Rollie Burroughs. Is he about?"

"Why no, Miss Gideon. Rollie left for St. Louis several weeks ago. I'm sure he'll be back in time, but as yet we have not heard from him as to when that might be."

Cecelia's face turned ashen and a tiny-gloved hand went to her throat. Stammering a tremulous word of thanks she turned the horse about and headed back out the lane.

4

OLD ST. LOUIS

From Idaho to the St. Louis stockyards, Rollie traveled in the railroad livestock car with his Palouse horse. Using his saddle for a pillow and a mound of sweet hay for a mattress, he alternately slept and lay pondering past years and now the uncertain future. He could not remember ever feeling so alone. Steam billowed from the engine, two short toots of the whistle and they glided to a slow stop. Rollie brushed the straw from his clothes, slicked back his hair and placed the wide brimmed hat on his head. Looking through the slats of the car door, he could see it was lined up with a loading platform and ramp. Quickly he saddled the horse, gathered his belongings and pushed the squealing door aside to be greeted by a yard worker on the other side.

"Hey there cowboy," he said in greeting. "Welcome to the big city. You can bring your horse down over here," and he pointed to the ramp. Rollie smiled politely and thanked the man.

From the look of the sun, it appeared to be mid afternoon and his stomach growled with hunger. He had no idea how to find his way out of the city and the big horse acted stiff and sluggish. He decided it best to find a livery stable, get his first hot meal since leaving home and pass the night. Tomorrow would be a better day. The yard worker directed him to a livery stable near the train station. Unlike the familiar quiet rolling hills and clear blue skies of home, this place smelled of stale smoke and oil with a hazy sky and the constant noisy motion of bodies and machinery.

What the hell have I got myself into, he thought morosely and headed toward the livery stable. An older man stood near the side of the bricked city street obviously intrigued with the unusually colored horse. Their eyes met and the man smiled and raised his hand in greeting.

"That's quite a horse you have there young man. I ain't seen one like him since I was a boy out west. Is that one of them Indian ponies?"

"Yes, sir. It's a Palouse horse from the Nez Perce Indians back home. I hated to admit it at first but he's one of the gamest rides I've ever had!"

"Yep. He looks tough alright. I saw you come from the train yards yonder. Where you headed?"

"I'm lookin fer family down Jefferson County way, but I'm not sure how to get out of the city and the truth be known, we're both purty tired an hungry."

"Come on with me. You can leave your horse and gear here at the livery for now. These folks are my friends. We can walk back over to the train station, get a good meal an then you can come home with me. I got a place over by the fairgrounds and I'll be glad to help you out. You an your horse can stay the night with us an we'll talk about how you can best get to where you're goin in the morning."

Rollie was greatly relieved for the man's help and allowed him to take control of the situation. A small Irishman, Sonny Ryan wore a little black derby hat and long sleeved white shirts. The sleeves, obviously too long for his arms, were gathered up in puffs behind black bicep garters. He wore dark pants with fine gray stripes and finely polished black shoes. Rollie could not decide if the little man reminded him of a bartender, or an undertaker. Neither guess was correct as it soon became apparent that he owned and trained a stable full of Standardbred trotting horses near the old fairgrounds.

Sonny took Rollie over to the Union Station, a magnificent new train depot, recently completed in the 1890s at a cost of 6.5 million dollars. They entered through the train shed, an arched structure covering 11.5 acres of tracks, walkways, steaming engines and milling passengers. Following the other passengers they made their way to the Midway, a passageway with an airy roof of glass and steel trusses. So intrigued with the mass and height, Rollie had to stop and turn round gawking at the ceiling while more sophisticated travelers chuckled at his antics. Finally making their way to the grand hall, the simple country man could only stand and gape at the sight before him. The appearance was that of a medieval building with 65-foot high ceilings, sweeping archways, gold leaf and frescos. High overhead, Tiffany stained glass windows flashed colors like dancing gemstones. In his entire life he had never even imagined such a sight; much less actually experience it.

Ravenous, Rollie followed Sonny to a restaurant located inside the main terminal. The Harvey, a colossal establishment, served fine dinners to hungry travelers and took great pride in their midwestern hospitality. Dozens of attractive young women in high necked, waist nipping, long skirted dresses scurried between the kitchens and diners with heavy food laden trays. They found a white clothed table near the wall and ordered steak, stewed vegetables and black coffee.

Rollie watched with mild amusement as a pair of travelers began flirting with the young woman who served them. When the flirting became too aggressive, a matronly woman approached them.

"You will treat the Harvey Girls with respect, sirs, or I shall be forced to have you removed from our establishment."

Taken aback, the men looked sheepish, dropped their heads and he heard one answer, "Yes, Ma'am. We didn't mean no harm, Ma'am."

She nodded stiffly and started to walk away. Amused, Rollie chuckled to himself. Glancing up he caught her intense stare and arched eyebrow directed at his wide brimmed hat. The smile froze on his face as he quickly chucked the hat under the table. Once again the woman nodded a stiff approval and left. Rollie wolfed down the hot food, paid the tab and followed Sonny out of the station.

They picked up their horses at the livery stable and talking the entire way, rode to Sonny's stable near the fairgrounds. After bedding the Palouse horse down in a clean straw filled box stall, Sonny led Rollie up wooden stairs to a cozy apartment over the stables. Mrs. Ryan, seated in a velvet rocking chair, rocked back and forth in rhythm to the flashing crochet hook she wielded. After introductions, she rose to prepare tea and sweet cakes for their guest. The outpouring of warmth and friendliness from the elder couple soon had Rollie relaxed and confiding the loss of his family and his mission to find them again. They listened with sympathetic interest and vowed to assist in anyway they could. Comforted, he bade them goodnight, went back down to the stables and found an empty stall to camp in. Rollie Burroughs had made his first friends since returning home and another week would pass while he explored the historic old city with them.

The sun had hardly started to rise the next morning, but the stable already bustled with activities of feeding and harnessing the trotters for their morning workouts. Rollie donned his wide brimmed hat and walked out to the track to watch. Harnessed to high-wheeled sulkies they trotted round and round, some individually and some in packs. Several stood out from the others, moving in a slower awkward, rolling pace. Rollie had never seen anything like them before, in that, they moved both front and back feet on one side in concert rather than alternating with the opposite foot on the other side. Sonny, who had been coaching the drivers and directing the exercises spotted Rollie leaning against the fence rail and came to join him.

"Well, my cowboy friend, what do you think?"

"I think I ain't never seen the like of this before." he replied with great enthusiasm. "What the hell do ya call that?" he pointed at a big sorrel moving past them with the awkward rolling pace.

Sonny laughed at Rollie's obvious amazement. "That's a pacer. Think of it kind of like some people being right handed and some being left handed. These harness horses come in trotters and pacers....simple as that." he emphasized "that" with a final slap of his hands to the sides of his thighs and leaned forward with a big grin and raised eyebrows.

Rollie shook his head and said, "Daaam! Cain't wait to tell Shelby and Purdy bout this one."

It took very little effort for the Ryans to distract Rollie with the wonders of the historic old city. Before the sun was halfway through the sky he had already decided to spend some time letting them show him around. Sonny introduced him to the sport of baseball with a trip to the Sportsman Park, home of the St. Louis Browns. Rollie thoroughly enjoyed the experience but that was just a little more than he cared to own up to. Probably not a one in the lot that could ride a green horse or rope a yearling, he thought to himself.

Sonny and Meggie Ryan met in 1903, the year that President Grover Cleveland came to St. Louis to commemorate the 100th anniversary of the signing of the Louisiana Purchase Treaty and the dedication of the buildings and grounds for the St. Louis World's Fair. Meggie was a clerk in the Louisiana Exposition's office and involved with the planning of the Fair. It was the largest, most spectacular fair ever held until that time, covered over 1,200 acres and represented 62 countries and 43 states. The entire population of the city dedicated themselves to the planning and services necessary to produce such an event. Scheduled to commemorate the 100th anniversary of the Treaty signing, it grew so large that a whole year passed with the construction and it finally opened in April of 1904 running through December 1. In that time around 100,000 people per day visited the site. Electricity, a new wonder, was used throughout the Fair for decoration as well as lighting.

Sonny, obsessed with harness racing, worked in a stable near the Fairgrounds track. They married in one of the churches on the Fairgrounds during the summer. During that year, St. Louis was also host to the Olympics and the Democratic National Convention. Meggie joked that the whole world came for their wedding.

During that memorable week Rollie enjoyed the world of harness racing and helped Sonny in the barns. On one fine day he even posed for a photograph sitting atop a high sulky behind a sleek bay trotter. For a few hours everyday, Meggie took him out on guided tours around the city and through some of the remaining palace buildings and gardens left from the Fair.

Most of the fountains and cascades had been demolished and the grounds converted to a public park. For the first time in his life, he enjoyed the luxury of the electric lights available in the stable and in the Ryan's home upstairs. He knew it was time to be moving on when he awoke one morning feeling melancholy and restless. Bedded down in the stall with the Palouse horse, he awoke with the animal nudging the side of his face and ear. Softly stroking the horse's freckled nose he placated, "Alright, alright. I feel it too my friend. It's time to be about our way. We'll tell them this morning."

The couple took his decision with regret as they had truly enjoyed the company of the unspoiled, gentle cowboy. Meggie packed him food and Sonny provided directions out of the city and the way south to Jefferson County.

"I'll be back through this way fer the train home once my business is done. I'll be sure to stop an let ya know how things go," he had promised them.

Finally out of the city, they traveled through rolling hills and tablelands of rich humus and red, clay type soil. In the highlands, they passed through forests of oak and hickory. On the lower areas and along the streams, sycamore, maple, hickory, walnut, oak, buckeye and cottonweed trees grew in abundance. Fresh water springs were plentiful.

After experiencing the bricked streets and bustling city, both horse and rider relaxed and gloried once again with simple pleasures. Rollie's mind began to wander and he reflected on the kind couple that had taken him in. Meggie's whole life seemed centered around the Fair, the Olympics, the convention and all the concentrated excitement of that time. She had had a purpose with her work and an importance that most women of the era never experienced. Before it started and after it concluded, she was never able to grasp anything else of equal. When she talked with Rollie of the times and experiences, her face became animated, her blue eyes danced and sparked with excitement. By the end of the day when conversation turned back to horses, politics, or other general topics, she sat quietly rocking, absorbed in the labor of her flashing crochet hook. She lived through her husband now and without him she would have no identity and no purpose.

Sonny, on the other hand, had a purpose through the lifelong love of his trotting horses and the drive to compete. Living a few great years of history did not ruin his zest for life afterward. He was able to move on.

I may not be an educated man, thought Rollie. But, I'm smart nuff to see a warning here. The only difference tween Meggie an me is, she already peaked an's jest passin time till she dies. I've lived my whole life passing time an still looking fer the peak. Too bad, sumbody couldn't jest throw us both in a gunny sack with Sonny, shake it up and when they dumped us back out, we'd all three be even.

5   *ANTONIA*

The King's Trace, an early trail, ran parallel to the Mississippi River and passed lengthwise through Jefferson County. Jean Baptiste Gomoche, a French pioneer, established and ran the first ferry across the Meramac River. The ferry completed the King's Trace connection between St. Louis and Ste.Genevieve, two of the first trading settlements in the area.

Curiosity stirred within Rollie as he stopped to query directions and history of the trail from the locals that he encountered. Although the original trail had long since been replaced with better roads and bridges, he strayed off course enough to still find signs of it during his journey. He happened upon the site of the original ferry and camped the night there before moving on. Laying in his bedroll in this historic location he thought of the travelers that had passed through over the years. Who were they? What was their business, their hopes and dreams?

The anticipation of coming home, even though he didn't know how it would be, drove him a little faster with each day. The Palouse gelding sensed his mood and quickened the pace. The further Rollie went, the less sure he was of where he was going or what he would find. Somehow, the town of Antonia, near Ste. Genevieve seemed right. As he neared the little settlement, fear conflicted with excitement. His hands began to tremble and he felt his voice quake when asking a stranger for directions. Once in the town, he found a café for the first hot meal in several days. The owner, Daisy, who also waited tables, served him a bowl of thick, steaming beef stew with homemade bread and strawberry jam.

"Excuse me ma'am," he inquired of her. "Do you know of a place round these parts called Yeager's Tradin Post?" The woman turned and measured him with what he guessed to be a suspicious look.

"I grew up near here," he added hastily to disarm her. "I'm jest wonderin if Miz Yeager still lives there."

"You don't look familiar to me," she declared. "Miz Yeager is a dear friend of mine. What's your business?"

"My name is Rollie Burroughs. She's my aunt and I've come back to find her."

The woman's face paled, her lips parted and she raised a hand over her mouth. Finally she asked him to repeat his name.

"Rollie Burroughs," he replied.

"You are truly Rollie?" she whispered the question.

"Yes, ma'am, I am."

She stared at him and rocked her head slowly from side to side in the struggle to believe what she was actually seeing and hearing.

"How do I know you are telling me the truth?"

"Aunt Durley raised me fer awhile. I lived with her above the tradin post. I run away when I was still just a boy. I don't rightly understand why ya look at me that way. I don't mean no harm to her or the family. I jest want ta come back ta see her an make my peace."

Rollie's words and his pleading demeanor disarmed the woman. Her stiff body wilted and swept toward him all in one motion. She slid the opposite chair out and sat before him at the table.

"Young man, your aunt grieved over you for years," Daisy scolded. "She never gave up hope that one day you would return. I don't know whatever possessed you to run away and it's not my business but I just thank God that you are here now."

A chill ran through him and with great dread he asked, "Am I too late ma'am?"

"No, no. But she is quite old and frail as you can imagine. She stays abed most days. I visit her from time to time and we pray together. I just saw her two days ago and she prayed to know that you were safe and well before the good

Lord took her home. Whatever made you treat that good woman in such an uncaring way?"

She might as well have slapped him in the face for the tears of shame and regret flooded to his eyes and he was unable to reply. He could only stare down at the empty plate before him.

"I don't rightly know myself," he finally whispered. "I really cain't remember much of anything bout those times…jest that I seemed to be so mad all the time. I jest don't know what about though, cause there's nuthin there but a big, black, empty place. I mostly been working on a ranch out Idaho way these past years. But strange things have been comin in my mind of late…. an Aunt Durley is there too. I had to come. It jest wasn't possible to not come back anymore."

Rollie lay money on the table for the meal and reached for his hat. "Reckon I better go try to find her now. I know I'm in the right place but things have grown an changed so much, I have to think about the way to go."

"I better walk along with you. No telling how she'd take a stranger just showing up at her door claiming to be her nephew. I'll go in and talk with her first."

Daisy jumped up, whipped off her apron and called out to the kitchen girl to mind the café for a spell. She walked briskly down the raised wooden sidewalks while Rollie led the horse in the street and attempted to keep her pace. Three blocks over and two blocks down, the buildings became sparse and vacant lots overgrown with weeds and grass predominated. Finally, going around the last corner, he saw the old trading post backed by dark, ancient oak trees and the breath almost left him. Three stories of unpainted, gray-weathered wood, it appeared shabby and decrepit. He could only stand and stare. When the woman realized she had lost him, she turned back with a questioning look.

"This is the place, but it's sure not like I remember," he shook his head in denial. "My Aunt Durley….she still lives here? Like this? Is she all alone in there?"

"No. Your sister is here also. She cares for Miz Yeager."

"My sister? You said my sister." Incredulous, he stared at her with widened eyes and held his hands out to her in a pleading motion.

"I'm sorry, Rollie. I should have said your half-sister. Miz Yeager took her in too but that was sometime after you left. Look, just stay here while I go in and prepare them. I'll let you know when it's okay to come in." She left him standing in the dirt yard, climbed up rickety steps to the porch and let herself in the dark space beyond the door with a "Yoo-hoo. It's me, Miz Yeager."

Rollie found a shady tree to hitch the horse and loosened the cinch. The gelding shifted his weight over to one back foot, cocked the other one and promptly fell asleep.

What a life, Rollie mused. It should be that simple fer all of us.

He walked round the building, looking up at dirty windows and rotting wood. The more he looked, the more he was actually visualizing what lay beyond those windows. New caskets, shipped down from St. Louis, were stored on the third floor. He pictured himself, a young child, playing hide and seek amongst the caskets with his friends. The second, or middle floor was the family's living quarters. A straight shotgun type room, it was partitioned into three sections, kitchen in the rear, sleeping quarters in the middle and a living area in the front overlooking the street. The ground floor housed the store. They stocked everything from groceries, canning supplies, dry goods, tools, light farm equipment and even maintained a small bar in the back of the store. Memories of the store began flooding into his head.

The sharp noise of a slammed door snapped him to the present and he turned back toward the front of the house. A woman, possibly around thirty, had run to the edge of the porch and stood poised there, both hands clenched over her mouth. Quite tall, and big boned, long blonde hair fastened at the nape of her neck, wisped in the breeze. She stared at him with teary blue eyes. He stared back at her, his heart thumping as though it would burst right out of his chest.

"Are you truly my brother?" she finally asked in a tremulous voice. Sweeping off his hat and holding it in front of his chest with both hands, he could only nod a response. She stepped down the rickety steps slowly and walked across the yard towards him, each step faster until she fairly flew into his arms with a wail. The moment, so emotionally intense, could not be endured without them both breaking down in sobs and holding each other in the tightest of grips. Finally he raised his head from her shoulder and through tear filled eyes made out the form of a small, frail woman supported in the doorway by her friend from the café.

"Aunt Durley. It's me. It's Rollie." The girl pulled back and he broke from her embrace, leapt up the stairs in one stride and stood before his little Aunt. He feared to touch her for she seemed so feeble. She ended the hesitation by reaching up both hands and cupping his big face between them.

"My dear, sweet little boy. It really is you. Oh, Rollie," she cried. Carefully he bent over and buried his face against her neck and they both cried.

The Palouse horse lazed away the next few days in a neighbor's green pasture while Rollie became acquainted with his newfound sister and made peace with Aunt Durley. To accommodate the failing woman, the living quarters in the old building had been moved to the ground floor. Counters, displays and old equipment had all been shoved to the back bar area and stood in dusty disarray.

The trading post, a historic site, had originally been a supply depot and rest stop for wagon trains traveling to Independence, Missouri. Local people called the route The Lone Star Trail. In Independence, travelers could pick up The Santa Fe Trail that connected Missouri and Santa Fe, New Mexico. The Santa Fe Trail was the main highway to the new western territories and was used by wagon trains, commercial freighters, stagecoaches, gold miners and trappers alike. With the advent of the railroad, the trail was eventually abandoned, but the old Missouri trading post and the woman who lived there still lingered on.

Durley Yeager inherited the property from her parents. The eldest of two daughters, she accepted her "duty" to stay on and care for them as they aged, as well as run their business. In the meantime the younger daughter, Mary Emma, married Paul Burroughs, a businessman from St. Louis and moved away.

With Rollie's return, Durley brightened and began to eat and move around again. She slept a good bit of the day but roused herself to question him about where he had gone and what he had done with his life. She loved the stories of the Clyatt family, Purdy, Junior, Matthew, Daniel and their Nez Perce family. A horse lover, she was intrigued with his Palouse horse and its history. He felt so proud to have been a part of it after seeing her reaction. His sister, Emilie, sensitive to their need to recoup time and heal, gave them space and privacy. Then while Durley slept, the two walked about the property and explored their new relationship. The conversations never came around to their parents or how they both came to be with Aunt Durley. Something about the subject felt of foreboding and neither would bring it up. That would remain for their aunt to deal with.

The time came when he and Emilie sat by the old woman's bed while she sipped broth and visited with them. He felt such love and camaraderie in the room that the story of his bad dreams spilled forth and the whole subject was finally there to be examined. Aunt Durley only poised briefly from the hot cup of broth. She nodded her head in acknowledgement but never looked up until the cup was empty.

"That was so good," she complimented Emilie. Emilie smiled faintly in return and the two younger people waited for her further response.

"It's time," she finally said. "Neither of you know about your family. This all needs to be told while I am still able. The time for me to meet my maker is very near…" Emile lifted a hand and opened her mouth to protest, but Durley shushed her. "Above all, my dear, there shall be truth and honesty between us. It starts now and my end is the first fact we will all face."

Emilie looked pained but nodded in acknowledgement to her Aunt's direct words.

"What I have to tell you both won't be easy to take, but the truth has obviously affected you both and perhaps its telling will give you peace. You both come from strong, brave pioneer stock and I will start as far back as I can remember so you can feel the pride of who you are and where you come from."

6   *STORY TELLERS*

Aunt Durley then began her long tale.

Even in the last years of her life, Marie Leclede could still remember that flag changing ceremony as if it had just happened the day before. Born on the ship passing over from France, she landed in the Port of New Orleans in the Louisiana territory with parents and three siblings. The family traveled up the Mississippi River to the settlement called St. Louis and made a new home there. Eight years passed and one day her father called the family out to watch the ceremonial lowering of the Spanish flag, followed by the tricolor flag of France being raised. She had to cover her ears from the noise of bugles, drums, cheers from the crowd and finally a blasting gun salute. An honor guard stood watch over the flagpole throughout the night and on the next day, March 10, 1804, the French flag was then lowered and the 17 star American flag raised. Another celebration of bugles, drum rolls, gun salutes and cheering crowds ensued. She remembered a small band of Indians who came to watch the ceremonies and afterward a dignitary addressed them. He assured them they would be treated as well by the Chief of the United States as they had by their Spanish fathers. President Thomas Jefferson, soon after, named St. Louis the capital of the new territory.

That time stood out in her life as being happy and exciting. Little else that could be called happiness followed, for most of her years were filled with loss and tragedy. Like other men of his time, her father worked in the caves, mining niter, also called saltpeter and lead for its sulphur content. Mixed together with charcoal they manufactured a crude form of gunpowder. The best charcoal was made from local dogwood, willow, alder, hazel, maple, poplar or linden trees and entailed heavy labor to search out and harvest. In great demand, the gunpowder as well as the caves and mines where it was manufactured, were greatly sought after. Indian attacks as well as occasional explosions made it a sometimes hazardous, although lucrative profession.

It was from one of these expeditions that Marie's father never returned. The mother and her four children were left almost destitute. Through some savings, the charity of friends and occasional domestic work their mother saw them through young adulthood. Over time the joy in life had been worn out of her and the will to live was gone. Once her spirit was dead, the body soon followed.

Marie found safe haven in a marriage to Carl Burroughs, the son of her neighbors. Recent immigrants from Hampshire, England they thrived in the new world. Carl worked with his father in the family business of "Rectifiers and Distillers of Spirits." Raw Whiskey was imported from out of the country and shipped up river from the Port of New Orleans in huge wooden barrels. After delivery to their business, it was then cut and blended for resale. The family home as well as the business was combined in one fenced compound near the river levee.

Soon the babies began coming, one after another. Marie had five in all, but the first four never survived infancy. Withdrawn and bitter the woman went through her fifth pregnancy resigned to losing another child. Born on a hot summer night, he arrived loud and complaining. A strong, active little boy, he nursed greedily and grew quickly. Marie was happy to tell people that he wore her out just trying to keep up.

Aunt Durley wearied with the story telling. She sank back on her pillows and barely whispered to Rollie, "His name was Paul and he was your father," before falling asleep. Hearing her last words, Rollie beamed. He and Emilie sat, one on either side of Aunt Durley's bed. Emilie smiled sweetly at him from across the bed, tucked the old woman's hand under the quilt and signaled for him to follow her out of the room.

"Is she alright?" he asked once they were outside on the porch.

"Yes, yes. She just tires easily, but after a little nap, I'll fix tea and a snack. She'll be ready to go again. Don't you worry. I haven't seen her so happy in...in...I can't remember when."

They both dropped down onto the porch floor and sat side by side with their feet and legs dangling over the edge. Rollie's Palouse horse saw them from the field and nickered to his master.

"He seems to be attached to you Rollie," she observed. "He appears to be pretty smart too. What do you call him?"

"I don't call him nuthin. I jest never thought bout no name."

Maybe we should think of something together...it will be fun," she said excitedly.

"Well, he's got those funny spots all over his face so I guess Freckles would suit im," Rollie mused.

"Ohhh, no," she wailed in mock anguish. I heard you telling Aunt Durley about your Nez Perce friend and how he was a gift and I think the name should be something dignified and special.

"Yeah, I reckon yere right but I don't have the first idea whut it could be."

"Don't worry, before you leave here that horse will have a proper name and we'll get Aunt Durley in on helping us."

True to her word, Emile's prediction that Aunt Durley would be perky after a rest and snack was accurate. She bade them both to sit by her bedside and resumed the story.

The City of St. Louis was constructed over an area of natural caves and limestone sinkholes. Raw sewerage drained into these areas and from there worked out to the Mississippi River. As the city grew, new construction required the leveling of the ground and filling in of sinkholes. As a result the sewerage began to accumulate and back up into stagnant pools. The mayor, John M. Krum, warned the city council of the danger but his words went unheeded until the spring of 1849 when a cholera epidemic swept through the United States, carried largely by infected immigrants. Upon arrival in St. Louis, the area was ripe for a long siege.

Citizens refused to believe their danger and thought the disease to affect only the poor and lower classes. The disease continued to spread and in the month of June alone 1,259 people died. Not only did the city council members fail to act in the face of the crisis, they all fled the city leaving the citizens with a collapsed government. Only the succeeding mayor, James G. Barry stayed. A public meeting was held and a committee formed to take command of the situation. None of their efforts could stay the disease, mostly because they just did not understand what fed it. Not only did the Mississippi River serve as a sewerage run off, it also provided the city's drinking water. One resident remarked about mud settling to the bottom of a drinking glass of water, but at the same time felt it to be "healthful." By July the average deaths per day was 150 people. Half of the populace left the city to escape. Finally by the end of that same year, the disease had run it's course, leaving over 4,285 dead, including Marie's husband, Carl Burroughs.

Their son, Paul, a smart, strong young man had helped his father in the family's whiskey business from an early age. He mercilessly shook his mother from her grief and withdrawal and forced her to work with him and his aged grandfather in the whiskey sheds. Together they came back from the disaster and in time the business prospered once again. As the territory grew, so did the demand for whiskey. Paul began to travel in an ever-widening circle, selling his product around the state. On one trip through the little settlement of Antonia, just south of St. Louis, he chanced to stop at a trading post where the proprietor lived upstairs with his wife and two lovely young daughters. In the year that followed, any excuse to travel south justified a stop at the trading post. Both of the girls, Durley and Mary Emma had wild crushes on him. But Mary Emma was the one for him and she eventually traveled back to St. Louis as his bride.

Aunt Durley's story was interrupted by a call, "Yoo Hoo. Where is everybody?" Daisy, the nice lady from the café, let herself in the front door and started toward the bedroom. Rollie knew instantly it was a good interruption because of the happy smiles that appeared on Emilie's and Aunt Durley's faces.

"We're back here, Daisy. Come in and join us." Emilie called out to her.

Daisy brought a basket of fried chicken and fresh fruit from the café and joined them to eat and visit with good friends. When she heard of the family and local history story telling going on, her eyes began to dance and she almost choked laughing.

"Daisy," Durley called out to her. "You have the best story of all. You must tell Rollie about the Indian in the kitchen." Daisy seemed a little muddled for a moment before catching the idea.

"Oh yes," she said. "My sister Anna and I were just young girls when our folks moved out here. The government gave folks so many arpants of land to come out and settle the territory. A few stray Indians were still about but we didn't have sense enough to be afraid. My father built a little cabin and then went to clearing and working the fields. Everybody had to help then, so he and Mama went out to the field everyday and it was my job to watch the baby and cook a hot meal at noontime. One day it was just too hot to keep the door closed. I was at the kitchen table trying my best to chop these vegetables and had my back to the door. That old knife was just so dull." She shook her head at the memory. "Anyway, this Indian man had been just standing there in the doorway watching. He was carrying a heavy, bloody looking sack in one hand. I jumped when I finally saw him but he wasn't even looking at me. He was looking at the food on the table. He walked over, snatched that knife from my hand and…Whack! Whack! Whack! He just chopped those vegetables right up and then threw down the knife. He looked over at Mama's wood stove and held out his hand to see if it was hot. It was real hot!" Daisy emphasized with wide eyes and a nod. "Well, sir. That Indian reached in his sack, pulled out a big slab of raw meat and threw it into the oven. He turned around and walked right back out the door again. I just didn't know what to do then. The baby was sleeping, Papa would be angry if he knew I left the door unbolted, I knew that Indian would probably be coming back for his meat and anyway, our dinner still wasn't cooked. So I just started working on those vegetables and pretended nothing else was going on. Sure enough, a while later that Indian came back, went straight to the stove and fished that cut of meat out of there. He put it back in the bag and drug it across the floor on his way out. He never once even looked my way. Course I had to, real quick, clean up the floor before our parents came back and to the day they died, I never told them what happened. An I never saw that Indian again neither."

Daisy's obvious enjoyment in telling the story was funnier than the story itself. Their day ended with a lot of laughing and lighthearted banter around the sick, old woman's bed.

Word of Durley Yeager's visitor and his Indian horse traveled rapidly through the community. Curious, one of the few remaining local Indians came by the next morning to see such a strange colored horse and say hello to the family. An elderly man, he was quite tall with long graying hair and dark leathery skin. He wore the cotton shirt and pants of a white farmer, but the soft deerskin moccasins of his people. A neckerchief was fastened near his throat by a round, handcrafted, metal slide. A bear paw design was cut out in the center of the disk and a small star etched above the paw. The women knew him only as Billy and that he lived in a cabin on a small farm to the south west of town. The local people seemed quite fond of the old gentleman because of his good-natured humor and friendliness. He bore gifts of fresh caught river catfish and an old clay bowl filled with chunks of oozing honeycomb. Handing it over to Emilie, he remarked it an extra special gift, "considering my people think honey bees a bad sign."

Rollie's eyebrow lifted a little with the remark but only until he noted a very definite twinkle in Billy's eye.

"An how's that?" he played along.

"Honey bee is cunning. She is greedy and wants to take every flower. Like some people, she takes all and does not want to share. I try not to think about that when I steal her honey though."

Rollie laughed with the old man and knew right then that he would like him. After visiting the horse, and discussing its heritage, they built a fire and proceeded to clean and roast the fish. Reminded of his Nez Perce friends, Rollie suffered his first twinge of homesickness and felt an immediate kinship to the old Indian man. Billy demonstrated a soft, almost musical pattern of speech, interlaced with gentle humor and practicality. A storyteller, with no one to tell stories to, he found an audience in the misplaced cowboy. Curiosity worked two ways when Rollie quizzed Billy about his tribe and local history and then got a little more than he intended, for the old man talked the better part of the day.

Early on, Billy noted Rollie's interest in the metal jewelry that he wore.

"Osage believe the world is made up of two parts - the heavens and the earth. All the people belong in one group or the other. Tsi-zhu people are of the sky and symbolize peace and harmony. The rest of the people are Hon-ga of the earth and symbolize warfare and protection. Designs on Osage jewelry show the clans. All of the clans belong in one or the other of the two worlds. Billie pointed a gnarled finger to the bear paw on his tie slide. "I belong to the Black Bear Clan," he stated with pride. "Hon-ga."

When the old man finally left, Rollie went inside to find his aunt and sister. Taking one look at his bemused face they began to snicker.

"Man," he exclaimed. "What a great old fella...but he near bout talked my head off!"

"Billy is noted for that," Aunt Durley said laughing. "But make the most of it because his stories are all true history

47

and soooo colorful. When he's gone from this earth, all those stories in that head will go with him."

"Yes, ma'am." He nodded thoughtfully. "He promised to be back again before I leave an I plan to take your advice."

Chapter

7   *THE OSAGE*

The Osage Indians are the only true natives of the Missouri territory. Tribes that imigrated later included the Missouris, Sauks, Foxes, Delawares, Iowas, Sacs, Kickapoos, Shawnees and Cherokees. In 1803 the Missouri territory was estimated to be home to more than 30,000 Indians. Local Indians were caught between neighboring tribes to the west and white settlers who crowded in from the East. By the time Missouri had been admitted into the Union, the combined tribes were forced by the treaty of 1825 to relinquish more than 23 million acres of land. But like the greedy honeybee, settlers continually crowded onto what was left of the Indian land. Despite complaints to government officials, little was done to protect the tribes and most were finally forced to the most southwesterly portion of the state. Small bands of warriors forayed amongst the white settlers in that area until Governor Lilburn W. Boggs called out the militia, thus began what was to be known as The Osage War of 1837. Overwhelmed by the number of soldiers most of the Indians were escorted to, or forced over, the Missouri state line. Consequently one group of peaceful Indians living in the Stone Creek area was taken to the Arkansas border with orders to observe the treaty agreement and never return to Missouri. Comprised primarily of family groups with women and children, this particular band suffered unnecessarily because their removal occurred during sometimes-harsh winter months. Shawnees, Delawares and Osage were the last of the tribes forced to leave the State.

Despite decades of skirmish and warfare, trade still existed amongst various peoples of the territory. Indians provided meat and hides, buffalo robes, decorations made from animal teeth and porcupine quills, in exchange for weapons, wool blankets, glass beads and other trade goods including tobacco, which they smoked in long stem pipes. They traveled to compounds, forts and even St. Louis to conduct business.

Auguste Pierre Chouteau and his allies largely dominated early fur trade between the western tribes and Europe. French fur traders enjoyed a profitable relationship with the Osage tribe and in many cases intermarried with them. A common practice of the time, they often maintained two households, one with a white "city wife" and family in St. Louis and one with an Indian or "country wife" and family in frontier compounds. Mixed blood French-Osage children were usually baptized Catholic and spoke French as well as the Siouan language.

Old Indian Billy admitted to being the descendant of such a union and boasted of fluency in three languages, French, Siouan as well as English. He recalled how women were often kept as slaves and in one incident from his childhood, had witnessed a woman sold by her own tribesmen to trappers for $600 worth of trade goods. The Osage women took pride in competing and often boasted about who made the best canoe, carried the heaviest burden, raised the best corn or married the best husband. In a solemn ceremony, new husbands presented their wives with a burden strap they made from uncured buffalo hide. The women wore it around their forehead and over the shoulders to steady heavy bundles on their back. When not in use, it always hung inside, near the lodge door.

Billy obviously liked Rollie and came to visit at the trading post frequently. Although he talked a little too much at times, Rollie really liked him too and was intrigued with his stories and the history of the Osage people. He only hoped to remember all of it so he could share with his Nez Perce friends once he returned home. One particularly bright day Billy arrived in time to share morning coffee with Emilie and Rollie on the front porch. He presented them with a basket of fresh dewberries and black cherries from the fields near his cabin. Aunt Durley was growing weaker daily and slept a good deal. The two were feeling a little down about her and were glad to see the pleasant fellow hobbling up the dusty, dirt road in his old moccasins. Rollie particularly liked the story of the Osage's origin and asked Billy to repeat it for Emilie.

As Billy explained, "There were snails that lived on the Osage River long, long ago. One day the snails were caught in a flood and carried down the river. The waters carried them into the Missouri River where they were washed up on the banks. Warmed by the sun, the snails grew into a man, whereupon the man returned to his native land on the Osage River. But the beaver now lived on the land and fought with him. A peace was made through the marriage of the man with the beaver's daughter. Their children became the Osage and called the beaver, Grandfather. Osage are more caring to the snail than to the beaver though," he added knowingly and then paused for a response.

Emilie, wise to his games, took the cue and asked the question, "Why is that?"

"Because it is hard to be caring when the beaver pelt has much value." He smiled mischievously and extended upturned hands as if to say...and there you have it. As the three chuckled over the story, an eagle shrieked overhead. Gliding on outstretched wings, he circled downward gracefully as if in an invisible eddy of air. The three watched admiringly.

Reminded of another story and with his forefinger poking upward, Billy announced, "Ahh, I will tell you now of the eagle. No-wa-tah was the only child of Chief Old No-Horse. She married a brave called He-ta-hah and they had a son, Little No-Horse. No-wa-tah went to the river to fish and lay her naked baby on the riverbank in the sun. A great eagle circling overhead, just as this one now circles, dived down and took the baby. She carried it in her talons across the river and to her nest in Halley's Bluff. The mother could only watch them fly away and then listen to the baby's cries. When he cried no longer, she threw herself into the river and was swept away. Chief Old No-Horse's seed was lost forever on that day.

"Oh my word," Emilie clutched her hands to her breast. "Please tell us that's just another legend, Billy."

"No," he replied sadly. "That one is true and was passed down through my people."

After the eagle story the happy mood disintegrated and Billy left soon after. The mood deteriorated even more as the two sat together on the porch with their morose thoughts.

"Rollie." Emilie broke the silence. "I am so scared for Aunt Durley. I know it is a matter of time and I just don't know what I am going to do without her." The further she got with the statement, the nearer to tears she became. She turned her head away so he could not see them. Rollie leaned close to his sister and put a burly arm across her shoulders.

"Ya got me now Emilie. I'm yer big brother. Remember?"

She nodded and gave him a grateful but weak smile.

"Emilie, why ain't ya ever married? Why are ya still here?"

"How can you even ask? I could never leave her here alone again. She stayed to care for her parents and then she was alone. The business petered off to nothing and she had nowhere else to go. I had to stay."

"Was there ever anybody?" he inquired gently.

Emilie smiled slightly and nodded her head. "Oh yes," she said and her sad eyes filled with tears again at the memory. "He is a businessman from St. Louis and transports grain downriver. He comes through here from time to time on the way to New Orleans. He usually travels by riverboat but sometimes he comes by on horseback just to see me. He said he would wait for me forever and Rollie, I love him with all my heart. But I would throw myself in the river like the Indian woman, before I would even consider leaving Aunt Durley. She took me in and raised me. How could I?"

"Does she know about this man?" he asked.

"No…and I don't want her to. It would make her feel so bad and I couldn't live with that."

The big man leaned forward in his chair, elbows on his knees and fingers intertwined. He stared at the floor.

"Okay," he said finally. "Yer not alone with this Emile. I'm here fer however long ya need me. An when this is over…when this is over…. well, we'll jest handle things as they come."

Tearfully, they stood up and held each other. Aunt Durley's cries, "Emilie, Rollie," ended the moment and they rushed back into the house.

8

NEW MADRID

After preparing and serving Aunt Durley's breakfast of oatmeal and tea, Emile helped the old woman bathe and dressed her in a clean gown and robe. The sound of birds chirping outside brought a small smile to Durley's face.

"Emile dear. Ask Rollie to help me outside so we can sit in the sun a spell. I want to see the sky and hear the birds."

"Yes, ma'am," she said excitedly and clapped her hands together. This was a very good sign and relieved the gloom they felt earlier in the morning. Carrying the frail little body in his big arms was akin to a father gently carrying a little baby. He sat her down on a pillow filled chair and Emilie tucked a blanket over her lap and legs. A pleasant silence settled over the three as they simply enjoyed the spirit of the morning. Orange breasted robins flocked in the yard, cocked their heads over the grass and dove at the insects under it. Little brown wrens chirped in the trees and a woodpecker tapped on the old persimmon tree. Aunt Durley lay her head back, closed her eyes and smiled.

"This is so peaceful," she sighed. "but we need to get on with our past. Today I want to tell you about our side of the family…. your mother's and mine." She smiled sweetly as if wanting their approval and they both leaned forward eagerly to hear her better, for these were stories they both longed to hear.

"From what was passed down, half our ancestors were French. Many of the poor French were sent out to build settlements and farms in the Canadian territories. I am told that our family was there over 200 years ago. While the British were advancing from the east, many of our French Canadian ancestors were migrating south down the St. Lawrence River and through the Great Lakes. Before long they were exploring down the Mississippi River all the way to what is now Louisiana. They first planted roots in this territory over on the east side of the river in a settlement they called Kaskaskia. As more whites moved west, the Osage moved south and west too. But those were dangerous times," Aunt Durley emphasized with narrowed eyes and a roll of her head. "The Indians raided and killed so many. I cannot imagine braving such a world. My mother told me stories of a huge forest…how it covered and darkened their world. It was not uncommon for children or even occasionally a grown up to just wander too far in and never be seen again."

Aunt Durley looked upward at the circling eagle that had returned.

"So beautiful," she murmured almost to herself. After a moment's rest, she seemed embarrassed to have drifted off and continued with the story.

"Anyway, my grandparents were the first of our family to cross the Mississippi River from Kaskaskia to a settlement they now call Ste. Genevieve. Of course Missouri was still a territory then and Mama said they never knew who it belonged to, what with the Spanish, the French, sometimes the English and then the United States in the end. And if that wasn't enough there was still the Osage. You never knew when and from where they would come round."

"French was the only language spoken in that household. My mother told me the first time she laid eyes on Papa he spoke to her in English. Well, she didn't have any idea what he was saying to her, but she liked what she saw. From that day on, she was determined to learn English."

"Now, my father's family, the Yeagers, came up the Mississippi from the Port of New Orleans. Grandpa Yeager had a homestead near the river in New Madrid. Some people don't want to believe what Grandpa told me, but I swear to you, this is the truth." Durley's eyes narrowed conspiratorially and she shook a gnarled finger at Emilie and Rollie to emphasize the point.

Anton Yeager loved the New Madrid territory. Being a minority German immigrant in a world of French inhabitants never fazed him. At times he awoke in the night and marveled how perfect life had become and the happiness he found here. He had a beautiful wife, Gerta, a little boy, Oscar, a 160-arpent homestead, two strong mules, a cow, pigs and chickens. Their first year, 1810, had been productive. With his neighbor's help, they cleared the first field, erected a simple one-room cabin with a stone fireplace, a livestock shelter and pens. The next spring he planted crops and harvested more than enough to see them through the winter. Gerta dried onions, peppers, corn and other seed crops and strung them in long garlands from the rafters. Next year promised to be better than the one before. The only other thing he could wish for now would be more children.

In the early morning hours of December 16th, as Anton and Gerta lay asleep in their bed, they were suddenly thrown out of it and onto the floor as the earth beneath their cabin pitched and rolled. Gerta grabbed and hung onto the legs of the oaken dresser only to have the upper drawers slide out and fall atop her. Anton struggled to his feet and held onto the bedpost as the floor continued to roll and pitch. The log walls began to split and break apart, emitting a sickening, cracking noise. The vegetable garlands hanging from the rafters swung back and forth wildly, while the heavier, rope-suspended lamp whipped around from the central beam in the main room of the cabin. Coal oil spewed from the lamp with each swing and splattered over the room. A grinding, vibrating, thunder-like noise deafened them and drowned out Gerta's screams of pain and terror. The horrible noise and pitching motion seemed to be unending. Gerta screamed it was the devil, come to get them. Oscar, sleeping in the loft, tried to climb down the ladder to reach his parents but was slung violently off the rungs mid-way down and crashed to the cabin floor. As the noise and movement finally began to abate, Anton could hear the screams of his animals and that of the wild birds outside. From a good half mile away, an ominous roar from the Mississippi River frightened him more than that of the swaying floor. Bruised and bleeding, Gerta threw over the dresser drawers that had fallen on her and rushed to pick her child from the floor where he lay. Just as she reached him, one last violent roll of the earth broke the weakened mortar in the stone fireplace and it toppled in pieces forward to the center of the room. Gerta screamed and threw herself over the prostate body of the boy just before the stones collapsed atop of them. Embers from the fireplace ignited the spattered coal oil and within moments the room began to smolder. With a strength that he never knew existed, Anton began raking and slinging the heavy fireplace stones aside and dragged his wife and son outside in the freezing night. Pitch black outside, the night air was saturated with the smell of sulphurous vapors. He dashed back into the flaming cabin again and again for blankets and clothing to cover them with. Then he sat in the sulfur filled night air rocking and holding them, one in each arm. Between that time and sunrise the aftershocks continued and in fact did not cease until March, four months later.

By morning Gerta had died, never regaining consciousness. A neighbor, passed through looking for his animals and stopped long enough to help Anton bury her on the hill overlooking the river. Oscar, in shock, lay trancelike in his father's arms. Before he left that awful day, the neighbor man, describing the great river, told Anton it was the most frightful sight he had ever witnessed.

"Why at one point," he exclaimed, "the water pulled back from its banks, and lifted upward to heights of 15 or 20 feet I reckon. Boats was just left stranded there and fish were flopping around on the riverbanks. Then that water broke loose and crashed back inland, carrying the boats, trees and anything that lay in its path," he swept an arm from side to side, dramatizing the scene. "The moon was shining and in just that short time I could see the riverbed underneath, with these great deep cracks in it and clouds of that awful smelling sulfur fumes was just belching out of them. If you go down near the water's edge you can still see where the fields are covered in wet sand that come out of those cracks." He paused, drew in a deep breath and said, "I feared the earth was trying to open up and eat us all."

Cold and hungry, Anton's mules returned to their barn the next day. But like most of his neighbors, he never found the rest of his animals. With the aftershocks continuing day after day, the frightened residents of the territory gathered what they could and fled. Like his neighbors, Anton salvaged what little was left and loaded it in the wagon. He harnessed the mules, gathered his son in his arms and headed north. It seemed they had traveled forever but the earth still moved sickenly with the quake's aftershocks. The mules froze in place with stiffened legs spread for balance and brayed in fright. The animals were no more afraid than Anton, but he held strong, talked to them and held their bridles until the ground grew still again.

But Oscar showed no reaction to any of it. He lay impassive, either in his father's arms or wrapped in a blanket on the wagon seat. A pallid face framed dark sunken eyes that looked through and past everything that came in front of him. When Anton held a cup of water to the little boy's mouth the liquid rolled back over his lips and splashed down the front of his shirt. Anton turned the mule team north on the trail and trusted them to find the way while he sat in the wagon holding and rocking his son.

"Oscar, Oscar," he cried with tears splashing down on the boy's face. "Please try my sweet little boy. You've got to try. I'm here for you and I ain't leaving you. Please Oscar. Come back to your Pa. We're all there is for each other now." But Oscar never reacted to his father's pleas, for he now existed in a deep, dark place where no one nor nothing could touch him.

With the sun receding in a pink western sky, the mules finally carried them into the little settlement of Antonia. One had lost a shoe and was beginning to limp on a badly bruised foot. The other, pulling extra weight began to trip and stagger with exhaustion. The only other thing that could make it worse happened, when the left rear wheel began to wobble just before they reached the settlement. He pulled the team up to the trading post yard and looked over the imposing building. Three stories tall of hard white oak and walnut lumber, the long, narrow building fronted on the dirt trail. River stone fireplaces on each end, at all three levels were topped with chimneys that rose high above the wood shingled roof.

Patra Lang glanced out through the front window in time to see Anton's wagon pull off the trail and into the post yard. The mules seemed about to drop. Their master barely able to stay upright, hunched over on the hard wooden seat, his arms encircling a blanketed bundle. For days the Langs watched earthquake survivors passing through on the trail, many stopping for supplies and leaving behind tales of horror and survival. Indeed, they had experienced the tremors themselves and marveled at the size and intensity of this quake to affect the land so many miles away.

"Oh my, oh my," she whispered to herself. Then calling loudly over her shoulder, "Martin, Martin. Come outside."

She stepped out the door and down the porch steps as quickly as her plump, elderly body would allow. She lay a light hand on the man's arm and he lifted his eyes to look in her face. What he saw was a sweet, caring, gentle grandmotherly lady with graying hair, but what she saw was a ravaged soul on his way out of hell. Because she knew where he had come from, there was no need to ask questions. His haunted eyes told her all she needed to know. She lifted a corner of the blanketed bundle in his lap and the child with the blank face simply looked beyond her.

"Oh, the little one," she whispered. "Give him to me" and without waiting she pulled the child out of Anton's arms and carried him into the building. Martin, who had been standing nearby, stepped up to the wagon.

"You're welcome to stop here for now. Come, bring your mules to the barn and we'll care for them. Don't worry about your boy; he's in good hands."

Once the wagon had been moved inside the barn, they worked together to unharness the mules and give them the first grain and hay they'd had for days. Lifting the bruised hoof of the one animal, Anton, released it again without even looking for the damage. Instead he fell limp across the animal's neck and began to sob deep wretched cries of agony. Martin busied himself elsewhere in the barn until Anton regained control, then directed him to wash his face and hands in the bucket and led him back to the post building.

The trading post was crammed with food staples, tools, wagon wheels, dry goods and anything imaginable that a pioneer family could need or want. The entire bottom floor of the building was opened into one big room. In the center stood a counter with scales and containers of beans, rice, coffee and candy. Toward the rear of the room, a small area had been set aside with a table and comfortable chairs for the couple to rest and visit with customers during quiet times. The room was chilly save for the family area where the fireplace was in use. Near the front of the store a tall fir Christmas tree stood covered with handmade paper decorations, ribbons and candy. Anton, holding his hat with both hands, stopped and stared at the tree. His mouth fell open and eyes of despair rolled toward the ceiling.

"What day is this?" he asked.

"It's Christmas Eve," Martin answered from behind him.

Anton dropped his head, rubbed a hand across his brow and groaned. Then turning, he saw Patra near the fireplace in her big rocking chair. The child lay snuggled against her ample bosom. His dark eyes were finally closed in sleep, a dried tear on his cheek and a little thumb in his mouth. Patra nodded at the table next to her chair for him to see a half empty cup of milk.

"Thank you ma'am," he said softly.

Aunt Durley paused in her story telling. The Palouse horse in the field ran back and forth, back and forth whinnying and calling for Rollie's attention. It became impossible to continue with his racket.

"Rollie dear. Whatever is wrong with your horse?"

"Well, I think fer one thing, he's lonesome. Fer another, I didn't feed him yet and the last thing, he's just got too much energy built up. He needs to git out an blow the stink off. I'll take im out fer a ride later today," he answered.

Emile chimed in, "I, for one, could use a cup of tea. In the meantime, Rollie, why don't you feed…feed…what's his name. Hey! We still haven't thought of a name for that horse yet!"

"Nope. We sure ain't. Got any good ideas Aunt Durley?" Rollie asked.

The old woman raised her eyebrows, thought a moment and replied, "I haven't a clue. But, not to worry, dear boy. We'll come up with just the right thing for him."

Emile laughed and jumped up to make tea, Rollie left to feed his horse and Aunt Durley, content for the moment, just smiled after them.

Emilie prepared a tray with tea, thick slabs of bread and a small bowl of her huckleberry jam. She lay the tray on a wooden stool in front of Aunt Durley's chair and handed out the tea in delicate old Bavarian porcelain cups. Rollie balanced the fine cup and saucer in his left palm and tried to imitate the women as they looped their index finger through the handle and lifted the cup to their lips. His thick fingers could not begin to penetrate the handle opening. A little frustrated he balanced the saucer in his lap, wrapped both hands around the outer cup and slurped the tea. He flushed deep red when he realized what he had done and that both women were staring.

"Scuse me," he stammered. Emilie covered her mouth with one hand, dropped her head and began snickering, soon to be followed by Aunt Durley. An awkward moment passed and then Rollie began to laugh with them.

"I reckon, I been in the hills too long," he supposed lamely.

"Emilie dear, please look up on the top shelf of the cupboard and get Papa's old coffee mug. I want Rollie to have it. It will fit his hand a lot better than these tiny teacups." They continued to laugh and snack until Rollie, remembering the story brought them back to it.

"Aunt Durley, what ever become of Anton and Oscar? Did the little boy ever git right again?"

"Yes, indeed he did. Old Patra Lang had already raised seven young'uns of her own and she knew just what to do with that little one. She loved him and nursed him along and he grew into a fine young man. Little Oscar was my Papa you know! Poor grandpa Anton though, never did remarry. He struck a home with the old couple and stayed on to work for them. Finally they got to where they wanted to give it all up and go to live with one of their daughters in St. Louis, so Anton took a trip back to New Madrid, sold all his land and used the money to buy them out. This here building and land is one and the same that he bought from them. It was a thriving business back then, but as you can see, there's nothing here now."

"What about your mother, Aunt Durley? You said her family came down river and settled in Ste. Genevieve. How did they meet?" Emilie asked.

9 *MARGUERITE AND OSCAR*

"Well, dear, when my papa got to be a young man he was restless and kind of hard to live with. So Grandpa Anton decided it best to give him a little wing and see how he handled it. The little settlement here was growing and he thought they should expand their merchandise. He put Papa on a river barge to New Orleans with a little cash for shopping to see what he'd come back with. What he didn't plan on, much less even know about, was the billiard parlors down river in Ste. Genevieve. That barge crew pulled in there and stayed over a couple days dallying in taverns an the like. Papa had no choice but to stay close, but he did do pretty good keeping the money. Whilst the others were drinking and gambling he went to explore the little town and see what was available to buy."

As Oscar strolled the dirt streets of Ste. Genevieve, he could not help but admire the neat, homes. Most were constructed of logs in a single story, rectangular shape. The spaces between the logs were packed with straw and clay mortar and then painted with whitewash, giving all the homes a neat, uniform appearance. Everyone there had a picket fence and as he soon found, it was more than for decoration. Cattle, sheep and hogs roamed the streets freely. Although the people were predominately French and French Canadian, there were also Indians, blacks and a number of those who were of mixed race. Everyone seemed to get along and they all worked well together. Since the most used mediums of exchange were bags of salt, bundles of deerskins or lead ingots, his roll of available cash to spend attracted a few eager sellers. Inquisitive, the villagers seemed happy to show him around and tell of their wares.

Francois Aubert invited Oscar to accompany him home for a sampling of the area specialties that he hoped to sell the young man. The interior of his house was rather dark and sparsely furnished. With the exception of a grand armoire made from black walnut and a gold-framed mirror, most of the furniture was simple and crude. A small crackling flame in the fireplace cheered him and radiated one of their few real comforts. Oscar doffed his hat and nodded respectfully when introduced to Francois' wife, Felicite. She smiled politely and complied when her husband directed her in French to serve them. Placing two pewter goblets on the table she poured a sampling of his prized wild cherry liqueur. Never really having the opportunity to drink before Oscar played, what he thought to be, a bluffing game with the Frenchman. Without swallowing, he allowed his lips to be wet and then licked them gingerly with his tongue. The sweet flavor danced across his senses and invited him to try again. This time a full sip and he closed his eyes in pure joy.

"Monsieur Aubert, I have never tasted anything so exquisite in my life. Will you sell me some of this cherry liqueur for our trading post?"

"Yes. I will be happy to provide this for you.... and would you also like to try our local beer and cider?" Soon the young man's head began to feel a little wobbly and warmth flooded down into his fingers and toes. With twinkling eyes, Francois and Felicite exchanged a private look of mirth. Although slightly intoxicated, Oscar was still aware enough to catch the look and immediately caught the meaning of it.

"Monsieur and Mademoiselle. Thank you for inviting me to your home... and allowing me to sample your fine beverages. If you will be so kind as to transport the kegs and meet me early in the morning at the barge, I will pay you in full."

As he reached out to shake the older man's hand, a young woman entered the room behind Francois and shyly approached them. Still clutching Francois' hand, Oscar's mouth dropped and he stared blatantly over his shoulder and beyond at the sweet faced, dainty figure. She blushed and hesitated, but Francois pulled back, turned and smiled at her.

"Monsieur Yeager. This is my beautiful daughter Marguerite." Like her mother, she wore a skirt and blouse made of blue cotton and leather moccasins. She clutched a warm brocade shawl about the shoulders, but Oscar's eyes never moved beyond her face. She, in turn, stared back at him with sparkling blue eyes that widened when he spoke.

"My family does not speak English, Monsieur. I will tell them of your pleasure to meet them," Francois said as he nudged the young man toward the door.

Anton clamped his teeth into the pipe stem so hard he felt it give. Upon examination, there were four new dents in it to go along with all the other dents from previous times.

"Oscar," he said with great restraint. "What were you thinking? Did it not occur to you that people who stop here for supplies can *not* make it to Texas or California on cherry liqueur or apple cider? *This*," his voice trembled with emphasis as he poked a rigid forefinger toward the floor, "is a trading post. We sell dry goods and groceries and hardware!"

Oscar grimaced and shifted weight from one foot to the other. He had spent a lifetime on the receiving end of his father's tirades but knew that it would pass as quickly as it had started. Anton was a fair and loving father but like his father before him, he did not know how to show it. Before an hour had passed Anton felt ashamed for losing his temper with Oscar and offered him a chance to try once more. After all, how was the boy to learn if he didn't get to try?

"Papa, I'm sorry I let you down." I promise you this trip will be different. You'll see."

The next month, Oscar bought passage on the same New Orleans bound barge as the last trip, knowing the crew would go straight to Ste. Genevieve again. They did not disappoint him and upon landing he hied straight to the Aubert home. Marguerite answered his knock and remained partially hidden behind the heavy wooden door. Snatching off his hat, he peered into the darkened space where she stood. Nervous and giddy, the two young people simply stared at each other and grinned. Soft brown curls framing her porcelain face contrasted his straight black hair and sun tanned skin.

"Qui est là," called out Francois. Without waiting for the answer he pulled the door open wide. "Oscar. So it is you. Please, please step in."

Later, sipping cherry liqueur before the fire with Francois, Oscar conveyed Anton's concerns about his purchases. Francois gazed thoughtfully into his glass, nodding his head to convey understanding.

"Your papa is right in what he says. We have many other things to offer here in Ste. Genevieve…like tobacco!…and apples! We have a gristmill for the flour to bake bread. What about the Boudin?" Oscar looked quizzical. "Boudin, oh that is our good French blood sausage or there is also buffalo sausage from time to time and what about bear oil?" The more ideas Francois came up with, the more animated he became, pointing a finger in the air and leaning forward in his seat. When the discussion ended, Oscar had purchased a fair sampling of many of Francois' suggestions. He would continue downriver to the port of New Orleans for hardware, coffee and other staples, then stop at Ste. Genevieve coming back to pick up the rest. As their business concluded, Marguerite peeked around the doorway.

"Marguerite," Francois gestured her into the room. "Parlez en anglais," he commanded her with a gesture toward Oscar. Oscar looked quizzically at the man. "I told her to speak English. She has learned something just for you."

Blushing a deep pink, she stared at her shoes and barely murmured, "Good night. Please come again Mr. Yeager."

"Goodnight Mademoiselle Aubert. It will be my pleasure."

Oscar left the Aubert home with a broad smile and his heart fairly singing.

After completing the buying trip, Oscar returned to Antonia and began the task of unpacking and stocking the supplies. Stern faced, Anton kept the pipe stem firmly clamped between his teeth while helping with the chore. The more he unpacked, the more his jaw softened. Things are looking better this time, he thought. He was especially pleased with the supply of bear oil, a delicacy, for it could be used for a variety of things. As Oscar placed his purchases in their proper place in the store, he became aware that some spots were quite bare.

"Papa," he inquired. "did you throw out the cherry liqueur and cider?" Anton bit the pipe stem and looked hard at the floor.

"No, Oscar," he said tersely. It pains me a little to tell you that it all sold out and folks are asking for more… I'm sorry for giving you such a bad time," he added lamely.

A new era had begun for the Yeager's Trading Post after that day. Father and son worked together with a new affection and respect. The trading post prospered and within the year Oscar brought back the most precious commodity of all, his bride Marguerite Aubert.

Aunt Durley showed signs of tiring with her storytelling efforts. Squirming a little in her chair, she grimaced in pain. Emilie reached out for her hand.

"Come, Aunt Durley, let us take you back in to bed. We can talk more later," she pleaded.

The old woman raised her finger. "One moment, please." Taking a shaky breath she finished. "This building here is the original trading post and Oscar and Marguerite were our parents. Your mother, Mary Emma, and I were both born and raised right here. We all lived with Grandpapa Anton. He was such a sweet man and I have to say that we had a glorious childhood here."

Without waiting for another word, Rollie bent over the old woman, swept her up in his arms and carried her inside to bed. Kneeling by her side, he clutched the old woman's hand between his two, big calloused paws.

"Aunt Durley, afore you fall asleep, was your mother, Marguerite, a teeny little person with curly white hair….an she used to be over by the stove cookin all the time? An was she really sweet an smiling at me all the time too?"

"Yes, dear boy, she was all those things. She told you stories, sang French lullabies and cooked gumbo and baked tartes aux pommes…just for you."

"Aunt Durley," he whispered emotionally, "I'm finally startin to remember things. She was my grand-mère!"

10 *PAUL BURROUGHS*

"Aunt Durley," Rollie spoke softly to the old woman. I'm glad to know about all my ancestors, but it's my ma and pa that I really want to hear about. I know full well that sumthin bad happened here an if 'n the truth is not known, I'll never rest again."

"Yes, dear. Something bad did happen here." she conceded. "In fact there were a number of things. But besides that, I want you to leave here knowing about *all* your family and how good and special and brave they all were. You have much to be proud of. Please indulge an old woman just a little longer," she pleaded.

"Yes'em." He smiled indulgently at her.

"Your father was Paul Burroughs and he came from St. Louis. Before the war he had a family business…. rectifier of spirits…. I believe he called it. Anyway, he had two special friends. One was a German man named Hessler and the other a mule trader named Pettigrew. Together the three of them took part in a daring raid that helped save Missouri for the Union. You see the state government was for secession. In fact, take a close look at this quilt here on my bed. Do you see anything unusual about it?"

In unison, Rollie and Emilie, leaned over the bed, their eyes searching back and forth across the quilt.

"We give up, Aunt Durley." said Emilie. "What is it?"

The old woman, relishing the riddle, chuckled. "At the start of the war there was a state flag flying high atop a pole over in Hillsboro. It had a single star and stood for an independent state. You see the people here were for the South. A company of Union troops came through and cut down their flagpole. But not before some of the ladies hid the flag from them and in fact one of them spent purty near the whole day sitting on it." With that she began to laugh so hard, they could not help but laugh too. "Those soldiers kept searching until they finally found the flag and then after all that, decided it wasn't a secessionist flag after all and let the citizens keep it. After that day, the flag was near worn out from being flown so much but the ladies still wouldn't give it up. They divided it into pieces and sewed it into their quilts."

Emilie's mouth flew open and she squealed with delight as her hands flew across the quilt top. "Oh, my word! Show us! Show us! Which pieces are part of the flag? How in the world did you ever get this?" Laughing, the three pored over the quilt top trying to pick out pieces of the flag.

"Okay," Rollie finally had enough of quilt talk. "Let's go back to my ma and pa. How'd my ma wind up from here to way off in the city with him?"

"Well, honey, during the war he was driving mules up an down the state with that Pettigrew fella an they stopped here sometime for supplies." Aunt Durley paused with a dreamy look and slight smile. "Oh my," she barely whispered. "He always rode this wild looking black mustang. That crazy horse wouldn't put up with anybody but your pa. And he was the handsomest man....so tall, with dark hair and blue eyes. He was tan and muscled from working so hard. An when he talked... his voice was deep and just made chills run through me." The old woman blushed, embarrassed for her lapse in front of the young people. "Me an your ma both fell in love with him...but he only had eyes for her. I was a little put out at the time but they were such a grand couple, I finally got over it. I was glad for her. No sooner than the war was over, he marched in here bold as brass and asked our Pa for her hand. Old preacher Folson married them and off they went back to St. Louis. It was a good many years before I got to see my baby sister again," her voice trailed off sadly. "You see, Paul's mother, your grandmother, was starting to fail and they had this family business down on the river front. Mary Emma, your ma, learned the business and they all worked there together until his mother finally passed on. By then our pa had passed on too, and she was getting purty homesick. Finally one day I got this letter from her. She was so happy. They wanted a baby for the longest time an finally she was expecting. It was you, dear boy." she smiled sweetly at Rollie. "Your pa agreed to sell the business and they was coming back here to Antonia to look for a farm. Oh, my word! Me and your grand-mère just jumped up an down and yelled we were so glad to hear it."

"Jest a minute. Jest a minute." Rollie interrupted. "Aunt Durley, you mentioned my pa's horse…. the black mustang."

"Why yes dear. They called him Red River. I guess he was named for the Red River area in Texas where Mr. Pettigrew captured him."

"I remember him. In my dreams….there's a wild black mustang. I must have seen him then….when I was still little. Do you think it's him Aunt Durley?"

"Most likely it would be him. There sure weren't any others like him about."

"Yes! Yes!" Rollie shouted. "Go on Aunt Durley. Please go on."

"Wait a minute," interrupted Emilie. "We're getting ahead of the story. Go back Aunt Durley. Go back and tell us about what happened in St. Louis first…before the war."

11   *THE MULE TRADERS*

The first time Paul Burroughs laid eyes on Will Pettigrew, he felt an instant kinship. The two men bonded at first meeting. Paul thought later it was almost as if they had known each other from another life or time. A tall man, well over six feet, Will was lean and sinewy from a lifetime of hard physical work. A mule trader, he raised and sold the finest Missouri mules on his farm just outside the city. Sharp blue eyes, and a white beard dominated a face tanned and etched from years of sun and the elements. He was soft spoken, but direct and Paul knew at once that behind Will's gentle demeanor was a man who could not be pushed around. I like that, he thought to himself. I don't have to guess where I stand with him, because he won't hesitate to tell me.

Once you got past the height and the eyes, there was nothing left but the attire. Will loved his old, stained, wear-softened buckskin leather pants. In cool weather he wore a matching shirt with frayed, ragged fringe on the arms, but in the roasting Missouri summers he conceded to cotton shirts. The hat that he would not be separated from, not only fit his head, it fit his personality as well. The crown, tall and cone shaped, had once been an attractive light tan. After numerous horse and mule spills, one pig wrestling match, and years of weather it evolved into various shades of mauve. The double strand leather wrap hatband was completely overshadowed by a wide sweat stain. The brim was just a little ragged on the right side, but in Will's reasoning it would still shade your eyes until four in the afternoon.

"In short, it should last me at least another 20 years," he told folks with a twinkle in his eye.

Over a period of years, Will and his wife had earned a reputation for breeding the best of Missouri mules. A hybrid cross between large draft mares and donkey Jacks, the mules were in great demand in the south for cotton farming, logging operations in a number of states, by the army and even as far west as Death Valley in California for the borax trade. At one time they had been widely sought for the westward wagon train migrations, but advent of the railroad diminished that market. In addition to the breeding operation they also bought, sold and traded the animals. In the early days of his operations Will, with hired hands, traveled with large herds of mules, horses and Jacks through neighboring states selling along the way. Depending on the area and the individual animal he could get anywhere from $50 to $70 or more per head. Smaller mules were of little use and he learned early on, that the larger animals produced by draft mares to be more saleable. As word spread about the quality of his mules, the need to travel diminished and buyers came direct to his farm. As the size and quality of his animals grew, so did their market value.

It was on one of the early mule drives that he met, Maribel, his future wife and business partner. Maribel's family originally migrated from the East Tennessee mountains to the southern Missouri Ozark territory generations before. Of Anglo-Saxon heritage, they tired of the mountain feuding and sought out a new, more peaceful life on fertile river bottom farmlands. Other mountain families followed and peace and prosperity reigned for a number of years until the day that a member of the Alsup clan and a member of the Fleetwood clan quarreled. One shot the other dead and a long, bloody feud ensued for the next forty years. At least two hundred people were killed before the two opposing sides decided to settle it once and for all. By now, non-family members in the region had taken sides on one family's part or the other, including Maribel's father. They agreed to finish the war on a flat plateau that lay between Bryant Fork and Fox Creek. Several hundred men battled for a full day. Finally a truce had to be called in order to tend the wounded and dead. Maribel's father brought the body of his son home to bury while the fighting resumed back at the battlefield. Whether they wanted to or not, the population of the entire territory was divided into one camp or the other. People were called out of their houses during the night and shot. No one was safe. Rabid with hatred, Maribel's parents forgot they even had a daughter. She lay in bed one night listening to her father raging in the next room.

"…..the son of a bitch died before I could get even with him."

Sick and disgusted, the girl decided she could take no more of it. Her prayers were answered in the form of a tall, lanky mule trader passing through. Maribel had walked to the settlement with her mother to pick up supplies when a small gathering near the stock pens caught her attention. Curious, she approached the group and found them to be engrossed in several large mules that were obviously there to be sold. She had heard of a man from St. Louis who passed through from time to time selling fine mules and horses and was intrigued to watch the dealing. She liked his looks and the sound of his voice. He handled the animals in a confident but gentle manner. Maribel's mother called her back to help with the bundles, but not before she heard the mule trader mention that he would be heading north to St. Louis in the morning. During the night Maribel packed her few belongings in a sack, left her parents a note and waited up the trail for him to pass.

The sky lightened in the east and thin shafts of sunlight poked through a forest of maple and sycamore trees. A little nervous she paced to and fro while peering down trail into the shadows. Misty white clouds puffed from her mouth in the chill morning air. By good light, she finally heard a clip-clop of hooves and the sneeze of a horse. Planting herself firmly in the middle of the trail, so he would not be startled, she waited for his approach. A black cloud of disheveled hair framed her small white face. She wore leather work boots, a rumpled cotton dress and for the chill air, a blanket was draped around her shoulders. The remainder of her belongings was clutched tightly against her breast in the little sack.

"How do ma'am," he said reining in his horse and looking a little surprised. "Are you alright?"

"Why yes, I am fine, thank you. I've been waiting for you," she explained. "I need to go to St. Louis. I heard at the

74

settlement yesterday that you were headed that way, and I am here to ask if you will give me safe escort."

Will's eyes widened and for a brief moment his imagination took flight. Hmmmm, he thought with interest, and then took a second look at the girl's resolute face. A piercing glint in her dark eyes left no doubt that this was not going to be what he first thought or might have hoped. A dozen questions came to mind but he dared not ask at the moment. She appeared to be a person that had been pushed as far as they could go and he would not be the one to push her further.

"Yes ma'am," he said with a quick tip of the soiled hat and an adjusted attitude. "I'll be happy to see you safely to the city."

He loaned her a spare mount. Still clutching the small sack in front of her, she rode the horse bareback all the way to the city. By the time of the journey's end, he knew that this brave, little spitfire girl was the only one for him and determined to make her his wife. Maribel was as short and petite as Will was tall and lanky. While Will excelled with the actual farm operations, Maribel had the business head. She was the only person in the world who could tell Will Pettigrew what to do and walk away. They made a formidable team.

Maribel never saw her parents or the Ozark farm again. In later years she learned that local citizens, finally fed up, pressured authorities to step in and end the feud. Fifty men, from either side were brought up before a grand jury and indicted for murder. Soon after, the Civil War erupted and the charges were quickly forgotten. The Alsup clan joined the Union and the Fleetwoods went with the confederacy, a good excuse to continue the killing. By the time the civil war was over, the feud was over as well, for the Fleetwood clan, as well as Maribel's family had been completely wiped out.

With Will's assistance, Paul Burroughs chose a matched pair of bay mules. Both stood well over 16 hands and had the power to pull any freight wagon that he could ever need. With business completed he came around the corner of a building, and face to face with a sleek black horse. The animal shied violently, ran a short distance and then turned to face him. His head was high, ears pricked forward and nostrils flared out with a loud, rattling snort. A long, shaggy forelock fell over keen eyes and half covered his fine boned face. Startled himself, Paul jumped backward and exclaimed, "What the hell was that?"

Will almost doubled over with laughter for the two had scared each other so badly.

"That, my friend is a real, live, wild ass mustang"

"Jeez! He scared the shit right out of me! That horse is crazy!"

Will broke down laughing again. "I had almost twenty of those wild things here not too long ago. He's the last of the bunch."

"Why?" was all Paul could ask with a bewildered expression.

"Well, it's like this. I was down in northeast Texas a while back delivering some mules to a ranch. The day we drove the herd in, they was roundin up this bunch of mustangs. They'd driven them up in this little box canyon an was getting ready to shoot every last one of 'em. Well, I knew Maribel would skin my head when I got home an she got wind of it, so I had no choice but to stop 'em."

"Why would they want to kill something so beautiful and harmless, like this?" Paul gestured to the wild horse.

"Simple. They eat the grass." I just told em, if they put away the guns, we'd drive them back to Missouri.... and so we did. Between breaking mules, we'd break a horse, break some mules, break a horse. They make snappy little cowponies and I don't have a bit of trouble selling them. This one here is the last of the bunch and he's a handful. You want him?"

"Thanks all the same Will, but he's not something I could ever deal with. Wild whiskey's one thing, but wild horses are something else again."

12   *RED RIVER*

Paul loved his new mule team. Huge, gentle beasts, immaculately groomed with gleaming hides, they commanded attention wherever he took them. They pulled his heavy freight wagon loaded with whiskey casks all about the city as if it weighed nothing. He further indulged his ego with glossy patent leather harnesses for them with brass buckles and trim. Although his father, Carl Burroughs, was long deceased the business still carried the name Carl Burroughs & Son, Rectifier of Spirits. When the time came for a sign to be painted on the new delivery wagon he consulted his mother, Marie.

"Mama you have worked as hard in this business as anyone over the years. Papa is gone now and new customers are confused with our name. Don't you think it time we make a change?"

Marie agreed and after that day the business was officially called Burroughs Family, Rectifiers of Fine Spirits.

Maribel and Will Pettigrew rode into the Burroughs' riverfront lot just in time to admire the new signs being installed. Beneath the soiled, ragged brim of his hat, Will nodded in solemn approval. He led a dainty sorrel mare behind his own horse while Maribel sat astride the wild black mustang. Maribel smiled and complimented Marie on the choice of name and sign colors.

Surprised to see the black mustang and even more so because the tiny woman was riding him, Paul simply stood and gaped. Ever alert, the horse stared back at the man through a flowing forelock. Sharp ears pricked forward, head high and nostrils twitching, he waited. Maribel and Will exchanged an amused look. Paul approached cautiously and reached out to stroke the shiny black neck. The horse tensed, rolled his eyes sideward and down at the outstretched hand, but never flinched.

"Wow. Maribel, I don't believe you're actually sitting on this nutty horse. Look at how he watches me like he's a rabbit and I'm a fox or sumthin. How many times has he throwed you before you got this far?"

Maribel rocked back and forth on the saddle in laughter. Swinging her leg over she dropped to the ground and handed the reins to Paul.

"Our gift to you, she said sweetly."

Paul looked skeptically from her smiling face up to Will's amused one as the horse pawed nervously at the cobblestone yard.

"He's made to be a one man horse and I worked him out just for you. It would be our pleasure if you would accept im and give im a good home." He raised an eyebrow at Paul's, still skeptical expression. "I wouldn't let my old lady on im if there was a danger…an I'd be embarrassed to say I was skeered to ride im when *she ain't*." he challenged.

From that day on, the only time Paul Burroughs was not astride the nervous, but game, little mustang he was sitting behind his prized mules on the freight wagon. True to Will's word, he was a one-man horse and bonded to his new master for life. His flat, lean body graced long dainty legs and high curved neck. A sprinkling of gray on the forehead between his eyes spread out over the years until his upper face was almost white. That was the only exception to a sleek blue/black color. With little debate on the matter, he was named Red River for the area of Texas that had once been his home.

13   *THE GERMANS*

When the oppression in Germany became more than he could live with, Gottfried Hessler gathered up his family and immigrated to America. The Hessler family was not alone, for in the three short years from 1848 through 1850 alone, over 34,000 of them settled throughout the city of St. Louis and surrounding county. The motherland, in a state of revolution, made their exodus to new fertile farmlands and the promise of cultural freedom irresistible. Not all were farmers. Some were businessmen, newspaper editors, poets, teachers and doctors.

Gaining a foothold in this generally unfriendly place was a daunting task. Still sensitive to issues of discrimination in their motherland, they now found themselves vulnerable to attack on the streets in this new country as well. Herr Hessler, and others like him, found support through Turnverein or The Turner Movement, a series of German clubs that was formed for social recreation as well as athletic activities. Many of the men trained in The Turner Halls for hand-to-hand combat and weaponry. They formed German-American militias as well as their own hunting clubs.

Some of the old time resident Germans looked down on the newer immigrants, but Gottfried and his wife, Johanna, paid little attention to them. They were far too busy starting a new German language newspaper, establishing their home, educating their children and mastering the English language. Language became a major issue when, on the first day of school, the other children taunted oldest son, Gerd, for speaking German.

"Dutchy," they called him.

Dutchy indeed, he thought and resolved to become better than all of them. He never spoke German in school again.

Of the five sons, Gerd, the quietest, most serious of the lot seldom smiled. The four younger boys likened to a family of flamboyant otters, tumbling, scrambling about and forever playful. Each one had musical aptitude and played multiple instruments. No matter where they went, a party was likely to ensue. Impatient with their juvenile antics, Gerd thought mostly of business, science and politics.

For all the minor class bickering amongst the German populace, one issue that they all stood united against, was the practice of slavery. In this new land that professed freedom for all, the hypocrisy was incredulous. After all, freedom from tyranny was the reason why most of them had sacrificed so much to come here. The bondage of other human beings disgusted and appalled them.

Gottfried took his children to Lynch's slave pen on Locust Street. The hopelessness, degradation and cruelty of what they witnessed took the smile from all their faces.

Gerd looked to his father with tears in his eyes and simply asked, "How can this happen here, of all places?"

His father lifted his hands in a hopeless gesture. "That is the question." he answered his son.

The boy never forgot the lesson that his father tried to convey that day. While the other sons married and went about their rowdy ways, Gerd stayed with his parents and the newspaper. Frown lines on his brow deepened from day to day as the political climate tensed with talk of secession.

Distraction in the guise of a perky little redheaded nurse softened his face and turned his thoughts. Of German heritage, Erika had clear white skin, the bluest of eyes and a fine turned up nose. She made a happy addition to the Hessler family when Gerd brought her home as his bride. She lightened his mood and brought a happy balance to the family's serious existence.

Erika worked at The City Hospital on Lafayette, just south of the business district. She loved her work and kept the family briefed on hospital gossip and politics. Although she did not have the privilege of knowing or working under the German doctor, Adam Hammer, his legacy impressed her greatly.

"He sure took this local bunch to task," she laughed one evening. "Why, I heard that he made them look so bad at the Medical Society that they wouldn't let the reporters in to cover the meetings anymore."

"How could that be?" asked Gerd, the reporter element in him suddenly alert.

"Well," she began with the enjoyment of his full attention, "you know how well trained and superior most of our German doctors are. It's from the training they received in the motherland. You can believe it or not, but some of these American frontier doctors have all of a six month medical education…and I'm talking right here in St. Louis! Dr. Hammer just gave them the devil about their low standards here. You've met my boss, Dr. Schmidt. Well, he, Dr. Hammer and two other German doctors are the ones who started the Humboldt Medical College right across the street from where we work."

"Hmmm," Gerd mused. "I had no idea." Can you arrange for me to meet this Dr. Hammer? I'd like to interview him."

"I'm afraid not dear heart. He went back to Germany. But you should make an effort to get better acquainted with Dr. Schmidt. He gets so upset about slavery and this talk of secession, that he's almost rabid at times…. a little noisier version of you, my love. I really admire him," she concluded with a sweet smile.

Gerd visited the riverfront on occasion. He savored the smells and loved watching while the riverboats from New Orleans unloaded passengers and trade goods. On occasion he even found something to report for the paper. One of his favorite places was Butler's Tavern and he never failed to stop for Mississippi catfish and a beer.

Crowded and smoky on one particular visit, he almost turned back in his attempt to reach the bar for a beer. The smell of food from the steam table buffet gave him incentive and he thought, to hell with it and pushed onward. With a filled plate in one hand and a beer in the other, he turned scanning the room for a place to sit.

Paul Burroughs looked up from his plate just in time to catch Gerd's eye and waved him over to the table.

"Come on, grab a chair," he called. "We got plenty of room for one more. I've seen you here before, haven't I? Name's Burroughs. Paul Burroughs. This here's my good buddy Will Pettigrew," he gestured with an amused smile at the tall, rough man lustily swigging his foamy beer.

Will gulped it down. "How do," he said simply.

Gerd could not suppress a grin. "How do," he mimicked their casual manner. "Name's Gerd Hessler."

The three differed distinctly in dress, speech and occupation. But their conversation took flight with the ease of comrades of many years. Talk went from beer and catfish, the weather, their occupations and was just touching politics before they became aware the tavern had nearly emptied out and the buffet cleared away.

"Holy shit," Paul declared after checking the big gold watch in his side pocket. "I've got to get back to the yard and finish up. This has been great. How's about let's do this again next week? Same time, same place."

The three agreed and Gerd left with a pleasant feeling of male camaraderie long missing from his work filled life.

The three new friends' conversations turned more political every week. With war growing closer, it seemed that St. Louis would surely lean to the confederacy. The new governor, Claiborne Jackson as well as most of the state legislature stood for secession.

"Gerd, it's on the streets that Lincoln's asked our Governor to send four regiments for the Union Army," said Paul. "You're a reporter, so tell us what's goin on."

"Yes, it's true alright," said Gerd with his most serious of expressions. Among other things, Jackson told the president his request was illegal, unconstitutional and revolutionary. He said he would not comply."

"Whew," Will whistled. "Sure as shit, this country's goin to war."

"I have no doubt that it will too," Paul declared. "What are you going to do when Jackson calls for you German militia members to join up for the south? After all, we're a minority here and you'd have to go."

"That's not going to happen," Gerd said with a sudden fierceness. "We'll disband first."

When Will suddenly chuckled in his beer, Paul and Gerd both looked up in surprise.

"Do you think that's all so dam funny?" demanded Gerd.

"No, no. That's not what I wuz laughin about," Will replied. I wuz thinking about those Dutchmen all marchin down the road that time with guns an breakin up that slave auction on the Courthouse steps. Talk about guts. Let's just give em all some more guns and they'll have this whole thing straightened out in no time."

Will's words were truer than he could have known. The German militia disbanded immediately after Ft. Sumpter was fired upon and subsequently reorganized as volunteer regiments under President Abraham Lincoln. Soon after, a steamer load of stolen Union cannons arrived on the St. Louis waterfront, compliments of Confederate President Jefferson Davis. Packed in crates, the cannons were loaded into wagons during the night and moved to Camp Jackson.

"I watched the whole thing from my back window," reported Paul the next day. "Word is they got their eye on the federal arsenal too. I talked to sumbody, said there's 90,000 pounds of gunpowder, 60,000 muskets an one and a half million rounds of ammunition. Those state militia troops out at Camp Jackson could probably take it. Just think what that'd do for the South."

The three comrades stared at their drinks morosely.

"What's to be done?" Will asked almost to himself.

After a short silence, "Meet me here tomorrow," commanded Gerd. Using both hands on the table to push himself up, he wheeled about and strode quickly from the tavern.

14   *THE ARSENAL*

"The President of the United States directs that you enroll in the military service of the United States the legal citizens of St. Louis and vicinity...for the purpose of maintaining the authority of the United States (and) for the protection of the peaceable inhabitants of Missouri. It is revolutionary times."

General Winfield Scott to Captain Nathaniel Lyon, April 1861

Every day, Mira Alexander rode throughout the city in her carriage. She always wore a black dress topped off with heavy black veil. Being blind, she depended on her driver to describe what he saw to her. The local citizens accustomed to the sight and sounds of her daily excursions paid her no mind. Unionist, Frank Blair just happened to be her son-in-law.

The day after the confederate canons were delivered to Camp Jackson, Nathaniel Lyon, a Unionist officer and associate of her son-in-law, disguised himself in Mira Alexander's dress and veil, then boldly toured Camp Jackson in her carriage. After leaving the secessionist camp he went immediately to the federal arsenal and began planning. Convinced that a takeover of the federal arsenal by the secessionists was imminent, he called a meeting with the Committee of Public Safety. Next was to call in the militia volunteers and execute their plan to attack the secessionist camp.

Gerd Hessler crouched on one knee and leaned onto his rifle, the butt planted firmly atop the frosty ground. Clouds of white mist puffed from his mouth and nostrils in the chill predawn hour as he waited. His regiment, formerly known as the Schwarz Jaegeren Hunting Club, received a late night call to volunteer for the arsenal. Only hours before, Gottfried answered the urgent knock on the door and hastened to waken his son with the news.

"Rouse up, Gerd! Ve must report schnell!"

Gerd dressed quickly, hugged his wife and tearful mother goodbye then snatched up his rifle and ammunition pouch near the door. He hesitated in the doorway a moment, and then turned back to his father who followed.

"Papa, I have to find Paul and Will first. No one will know to notify them and they want to fight with us."

"Ach!," the old man threw up his hands. "Gehen Sie! Gehen Sie! Yust go. I vill find dem. Machs gut mein Sohn."

"Danke, hervorbringen," Gerd replied in a thick voice, then hastened into the dark night. Hours passed while, at the Arsenal grounds, he waited with the number of other volunteers increasing at a remarkable rate. By mid morning he was gladdened and relieved to see his father and friends searching the masses for him. They were together now and the time for action had come.

Divided into six columns, the army of over 5,000 men marched separate routes toward Camp Jackson and Daniel Frost's pro-Confederate militia. The camp was quickly surrounded and a gun battery installed overlooking the field. Vastly outnumbered, Frost surrendered within 30 minutes and his troops taken prisoner.

Over 600 of the prisoners were rounded up and began the six mile escorted march back to the Arsenal. Crowds of angry citizens milled about the streets and began harassing the Federal troops.

"Dam Dutch! Dam Dutch!" they shouted amongst other insults. Garbage and bricks flew at the troops as the mob, increasingly agitated, pressed in closer. As the procession moved down Olive Street the threatening crowd completely encircled the columns of Regulars and their prisoners.

Gerd flicked nervous glances at his comrades as he backed up protectively to Gottfried. Paul raised the rifle half way to his shoulder, a finger curled around the trigger. Feeling hard, cold and emotionless, the noise and contorted faces circled around him while time slowed to a dreamlike speed. He felt disassociated from what was real. At that moment he was keenly aware that he could deal with any threat or violent act that was thrust upon him with no hesitation. It felt good! Will stood squarely beside him as they faced the crowd. Towering over the others, his narrowed eyes glinting icy daggers; he fairly dared them to attack.

"Bring them on," he growled and patted his rifle in warning.

An assailant within the crowd fired at the column, killing the German company commander, Captain Constantine Blandowski. Staccato explosions of sound and white clouds rose above the nervous troops as they opened return fire into the mob. After the last volley, at least thirty lay dead with countless wounded. For a brief, shocked moment the streets fell silent. Just as quickly, a chorus of screaming, moaning and shouted orders to regroup ensued. The militia, with prisoners intact, fell back into columns and nervously continued their march through narrow city streets. Before those in the rear could even see the Arsenal gates ahead, the sound of German music within the grounds welcomed them to safety. Not one of the four comrades ever spoke of the shooting that day, nor whether they had been one to pull a trigger.

Erika Hessler came home with the news that her supervisor, Dr. Ernst Schmidt, had joined the Second Missouri regiment as surgeon. With 1,800 men under his care he had begun collecting supplies and equipment for the battles to come. Gathered around the Hessler supper table they listened intently to Erika's recount of the unfolding situation.

"I knew that Dr. Schmidt was upset about something. But I only found out today what it was about. They could only afford to budget him $66 to set up his whole field hospital. $66! Can you *imagine*?" She paused and gazed down at her plate a moment and then asked in a soft, deliberate voice, "Did anyone hear of the train robbery just outside the city yesterday?" She looked from face to face around the table with her question.

Johanna laid her fork across the plate, daintily picked the napkin from her lap and nervously dabbed at her mouth with it. Gottfried leaned forward intently, his left eyebrow raised.

"Vhut happened?" he demanded.

"It was Dr. Schmidt," she lowered her voice conspiratorially. "Some of his soldiers did it. They took money from the passengers and told them it was a forced levy for the war. The money went for medical supplies."

When she next looked at Gerd across the table their eyes locked in the sad, deep knowledge that more was to come. The look that passed between them was not lost on Johanna and Gottfried. Gottfried raised his glass. "Mai Gottuhr uber unserer familie."

The next meeting of the three comrades at Butler's Bar was also a solemn occasion. Gerd announced that Erika would be serving and traveling with Dr. Schmidt's field hospital. Gerd's volunteer regiment would be leaving for active duty within the week and the couple's final farewell had been agony.

"What about you two?" he asked solemnly. "Are either of you joining up?"

"I can best serve by supplyin Mr. Lincoln with the best and the most mules that I can," Will answered resolutely. "That's my callin."

Gerd looked to Paul.

"I'll be working with Will," Paul answered the unasked question. He'll be needin help to deliver 'em and I'm sure there'll be a need for my whiskey to boot. We'll be supplying the troops with whatever it takes to get through this."

The next day, Gerd showed up unexpected at Paul's rectifier shed. Struggling with the lid on one of the heavy wooden casks, he looked up in surprise when Gerd called his name.

"Gerd. What a surprise." Paul's quick smile faded when he looked into the solemn face of his friend. Hastily he stepped toward the door, wiping soiled hands on his heavy canvas work apron. Reaching out to shake hands, he was taken aback by the rifle that Gerd extended instead. Gerd obviously struggled with emotion and found it difficult to speak while his friend looked intently into his face and waited.

"Paul…my good friend. I want you to keep this for me. Soon I will be leaving and if I don't make it back…. I want you to have it." Paul opened his mouth to protest but a look at Gerd's face silenced him.

"We do not have little ones," he explained. "My parents are old and my brothers will not appreciate this." He gestured to the elaborately engraved, handcrafted weapon. Our hunting club, the Schwarz Jaegeren, sent money back to the motherland to have these custom made. Each member has an identical rifle." His gaze dropped down to the gun as he pressed it into Paul's outstretched hands. Looking up with a weak smile he attempted to lighten the mood.

"Of course, when I come back you'll have to give it up, so don't get too attached." He turned quickly and strode from the work shed.

Soon after, the three friends parted company and from that day, no one ever heard from or about the Hessler family again.

"Rather than concede to the State of Missouri for one single instant the right to dictate to my Government in any matter however unimportant, I would see you, you, you and every man, woman, and child in the state dead and buried. This means war."

Brigadier-General Nathaniel Lyon to Missouri Governor Claiborne Jackson, Sterling Price and Frank Blair, June 1861. *(Note: Nathaniel Lyon was promoted to General in May 1861. He was killed in the battle of Wilson's Creek August 10, 1861.)*

15 *THE FARM*

Durley's account of the three friends parting ended with Rollie staring sullenly at the floor. Even Emilie exhibited a gloomy response.

"Rollie? Emilie?" her voice trailed off puzzled.

"You know what, Aunt Durley?" he started. "It sounds to me like my Pa was somethin of a coward. I kin understand that Pettigrew fella with the mules but that doesn't say much fer my Pa."

"You are absolutely right." She stated brightly. "And that's exactly what most folks thought too. But the truth was that your Pa and Will Pettigrew not only delivered whiskey and mules to the battle areas. They also gathered information for the Union and passed it on."

"Yere saying my Pa was a Yankee spy?" Rollie leaned forward, his eyes growing big.

"That's exactly what I am saying," she smiled back at him. "Almost just before the war was over though, they got caught up in a skirmish over near Alabama way and Mr. Pettigrew was killed. Your Pa was wounded but managed to tie his friend across one of the mules and led it all the way back home to Miz Maribel. She buried him on his own farm and then she nursed your Pa back to where he could get on home to St. Louis. Not long after that the war was over an that's when he came back to Antonia and married my sister…. your Ma. He took her back to his home, his mother and his business in St. Louis.

"Whew," Rollie exhaled a big sigh and slumped back in the chair.

Paul and Mary Emma kept only the furniture and personal belongings that would fit on the freight wagon. Red

River, tied to the back of the wagon, trailed behind. Everything else, including the rectifier business had been sold and he now turned the mules south toward Antonia. Although Mary Emma was growing heavy with the expected baby, they still planned to be settled in with family before its arrival.

When she first started pressuring him to move south, he resisted. This was his family's business…. the little world that they had carved out with hard work and perseverance. His parents and grandparents were buried and had a history here. But still a nagging part of him sympathized with the fact that she was homesick for the peace of her own small community as well as for her mother and sister. St. Louis was never the same after the loss of his two good friends, Will and Gerd and his mother soon after that. Of course other people passed in and out of his life, but Butler's Tavern, the Arsenal, the city streets had all lost their appeal for him. Somehow his day-to-day life seemed tinged with melancholy. One gloomy day, the rumor of a farm for sale in Antonia caught his ear. The idea appealed and he actually felt a little pleasure at the thought of living on a farm. But when Mary Emma announced that she was finally pregnant, there were no second thoughts for either of them.

The farm lay only 5 short miles from the trading post. It was 170 acres inside Jefferson County and bordered by Rock Creek on one side. They started with a small two-room cabin that served as a crude home until Paul had a fine new house constructed. He included three bedrooms upstairs for all the children he and Mary Emma hoped to have. Downstairs was their bedroom, the parlor a winter kitchen and just outside, a summerhouse complete with wood stove for hot weather cooking. A springhouse over the creek bank provided a cool place for their perishables.

The first five years in the new home passed quickly, for every day was filled with planning, building and satisfying accomplishments. Little Rollie did not stay little for long. Big boned and heavy set, he stood taller and outweighed all other children his age in the area.

"I cannot imagine which side of the family this child takes after," declared Grand-mére Yaeger. "Do you think it has to do with his mother breathing all those fumes from the rectifying sheds?" she asked with a sly twinkle in her eye.

The boy adored his father and screamed when not allowed to shadow him about the farm. Paul held him against his stomach and chest with one strong arm while astride Red River. When Rollie was finally able to balance himself and hang onto the mustang's unruly mane alone, his father entrusted the horse to follow along in his nervous little pitty-pat gait with the boy astride.

"He's little Rollie's nursemaid," Paul bragged about the horse. "Nobody else kin even touch that horse, but he carries our baby around the farm like his life depended on it."

"His life does depend on it." Mary Emma said with a reproving scowl.

On Rollie's sixth birthday, Mary Emma announced that she was finally expecting again. The family rejoiced for it did not seem their life could get better than this.

16

WEAVER

The story telling had taken on a new feel. Rollie lay rigid in his bed, arms crossed behind his head. He stared at the black, indiscernible ceiling and wondered why he suddenly felt so cross and unsettled. Maybe I been shut up in this old building with the wimmen too long he rationalized. The truth that he could not admit was his fear of hearing the end of the story. The lone window in his second story room slowly materialized as the black outside began fading to gray. With an abrupt burst of anger he flung back the cover, rolled to the floor and began fumbling for his clothes. Thoughts flowed in rhythm with his frenzied dressing motions. I've got to get *out*, as one foot plunged into the pants leg....fer a *spell*, as the other foot was thrust downward. He cursed silently at the creaking stairs, then across the creaking floorboards, slowly opened the complaining door and ended safely on the porch with boots and hat in hand. He strode briskly across the yard toward the pen where the big Palouse horse waited. A slight chill hung in the air. He looked to the fading stars in the sky and realized that autumn would soon be upon them. A wave of homesickness flowed over him as he lay hands on the softly nickering horse.

"You feel it too, don't ya boy? Let's get the hell out of here fer a spell an blow off the stink."

He led the horse to the porch where his saddle and gear lay under cover. Jerking the cinch tight, he swung up onto the horse's back and eased quietly out of the yard. On reaching the dirt road, he had only to lean forward, with loosened reins to send the horse galloping recklessly into the gray beyond.

Aunt Durley lay silently in her bed listening as the man arose and made his get away. My poor, poor boy, she thought. You're still running away.

Old Indian Billy told Rollie on a previous visit where he lived. When Rollie finally reined the horse in, he found himself on the road that led to Billy's cabin. He pushed onward until they entered a clearing in the woods where the little log cabin stood. The logs had faded to an ash gray and appeared ready to crumble from age. The wood shingle roof also appeared rotten with gaping holes. But the rock chimney stood tall through the shambles, emitting smoke from Billy's fireplace within. Beyond the clearing and through the trees, his untended fields lay dormant

"Hello. Hello, Billy," he called with no response. His boot heels clumped loudly on the wooden porch as he crossed over and peered around the half opened door. The single room stood empty. He backed out and sat on the porch edge to wait while the horse grazed in the clearing. An hour passed before the old man ambled noiselessly from the forest, a freshly killed rabbit hanging from his belt. His greeting seemed flat but his expression told Rollie different. Billy was glad to see him.

They cleaned the rabbit and while it roasted over the fire they talked the early morning away. Billy related another of his favorite stories about the Osage people. This was of a small delegation from his tribe, who agreed to be taken to France for exhibition. It began as a grand adventure for the three men and two women. Starting from St. Louis, they traveled down the Mississippi River by steamboat to New Orleans, whereupon they were placed on an ocean sailing ship for Europe. Early on, they were a great novelty and treated royally with every consideration. Oft times, those who would see the Indians had to purchase tickets. In time, their mentor became bored and simply deserted them in the foreign country. They wandered throughout Europe for several years, alone and friendless. Eventually they made return passage to their home through the donations of several benefactors. Rollie, feeling a little like a foreigner himself on this day, related sympathy for their predicament.

"I cain't imagine jest wandering around, not knowin anybody, not havin any money, and worst of all, not speakin the languages." How do you think they even survived?"

Billy agreed but pointed out "They were brave and clever Osage after all."

Between rushes of insignificant conversation and Billy's endless story telling, Rollie finally lapsed into stony silence and stared at the ground, seemingly deep in thought.

"You are troubled, friend. How can I help you?"

"Aw, I jest don't know, Billy. Aunt Durley is telling me bout our family un I know this last part's not sumthin I want to hear. It's about what happened to my Ma an Pa. I should remember it, but I jest cain't...probably cause I don't want to. Anyway," he tried to say on a brighter note, "she keeps telling bout all these Missouri mules some of the folks had, an it kind of makes me want to have one."

Billy, although amused, asked in a serious tone, "What do you need the mule for?"

"I reckon I don't need it fer nuthin. I jest want to have one. I 'll probably take it home with me once I go back." He laughed, a little amused at the thought. "I got me a moonblind buckskin named Booger, a wild black mustang, a Palouse horse with no name and it seems like a Missouri mule would top it off jest right." He looked at Billy for approval.

The old man nodded in seemed understanding and then asked, "Why does the horse have to have a name? Isn't it good enough to just call him the Palouse?"

"Nope. It's not. Those wimmen are naggin me plumb to death bout a name fer this horse but nothing seems right. When I hear it, I'll know it. You know where a man might buy a good Missouri mule, Billy?"

"Just so happens I do," the old man answered with a broad smile.

By midday, Rollie rode back into the trading post yard leading a huge sorrel mule.

"His name is Weaver," he told the women lamely.

"Is that ole Indian Billy's mule?" Aunt Durley asked suspiciously. When he nodded affirmation, she looked disgusted, said "Oh my God," and hobbled back toward her bed. Emilie followed with a nervous glance over her shoulder.

Well…shit! he thought crossly. I got myself this great looking animal an have to come back an listen to sumthin like that. Now I know why I stayed a bachelor. This was the first time he had felt anything close to real anger since returning to Antonia and he wasn't sure why. A thought flashed through his mind that perhaps the mixed emotions had to do with the fear of hearing certain truths, rather than his irritation with the women. With that new thought he grew angrier still.

"An I'm sick of havin to mind what I say all the time. Cussin is good fer a man's soul an I cain't even do that round here," he said to no one in particular. He jerked angrily at the Palouse's cinch strap while his head swirled with irritation. A quick movement from the corner of his eye caused him to whirl and duck. A gaping mouth with long, green stained teeth encompassed his entire shoulder. A quick reflex was all that saved him from the crushing bite. The teeth raked through his shirt and outer skin and clashed together with a sickening crack.

"You som bitch!" he screamed. The exploded curse appeared to blow him in reverse as he stepped back from the animal. "Shit!" he exploded again and slammed his hat onto the ground. "Now ya made me cuss so's they'd hear me." If it were possible for a mule to have an expression, Weaver's would have been one of quiet amusement.

When Rollie finally found the courage to come indoors he walked with a marked limp.

"What happened to your foot," Emilie asked with concern.

"Nuthin much," he answered meekly. "The mule jest stepped on it."

"Well, he didn't do it on purpose, did he?"

"I 'spect so, cause then he wouldn't move off'n it."

For the next few days Aunt Durley waited patiently while Rollie used his mule battle to avoid her. The next bite cost him a front shirt pocket and teeth scrapes on the chest. It also brought him memories of Cecelia and how she used to mend all of his torn shirts. Homesickness added to his burden of emotion. The next day brought a rib bruising attack when Weaver swung his full body weight around and slammed Rollie against the fence. A lightning backward kick to the thigh finally brought the big man to his knees. He picked himself up ranting, cussing and sharply slapping the dust from his clothes. At least out here in the open there weren't any women to hear him blow off.

"Reckon if I put a bullet tween your gawl dam eyes you'd stop being so hateful, you big sack 'o shit." He shook a finger roughly at the mule, his hair flying and face reddened. "That'd be too easy though. It's you 'n me Weaver!" he shouted.

Rollie turned and limped toward the fence. Weaver, with flattened ears and mouth agape with teeth flashing, charged the man's back. Before Rollie could even react, the powerful Palouse horse let fly with both back hooves as Weaver passed behind him. Both hooves connected squarely in the mule's ribcage and lifted him fully off the ground. He crashed down on his opposite side and lay stunned. Rollie looked from one to the other.

"Dam!" was all he could say.

A few moments passed before the mule finally raised his head, looked around and then rose up on his front feet. He strained momentarily, then scrambled to all fours, shook off the dust and looked back at the two staring at him. Weaver stood subdued and humiliated.

When Indian Billy came the next morning to visit he brought them gifts of persimmons and blackberries. They gave him coffee and shared easy talk until his curiosity could not be contained any longer. Finally, he casually asked if Rollie were happy with the great mule that he had sold him. The women broke into peals of laughter and Rollie simply looked disgusted.

After relating his trials with Weaver and the final showdown with the Palouse horse, Billy did not hesitate.

"It was meant to be," he said convincingly. "You needed a name for the Palouse horse and the mule gave you one." Rollie's face began to redden but Billy seemed not to notice.

"I told you that my people believe the world is made of two parts – the heavens and the earth." He looked from face to face as if questioning that they remembered. Emilie said yes for all of them so he would get on with it. All people belong in one world or the other. Tsi-zhu people are of the sky and symbolize peace and harmony. Hon-ga people are of the earth and symbolize warfare and protection. Palouse is the warhorse of the Nez Perce people. He was your gift from them and he protects you." Billy paused and then looked solemnly to Rollie. His name is Hon-ga." This time they all laughed together and agreed it was the perfect name for Rollie's Palouse horse.

Later that night Aunt Durley became ill and collapsed. Emilie ran frantically for the doctor, but in her heart she feared there was little to hope for.

17 *BLACK DAYS*

"Your aunt is failing. I cannot predict how long she can last, but then she might still fool me and rally again," Doc Williams told them. A distinguished looking gentleman with tanned skin, white hair and soft brown eyes he looked kindly at Rollie. Doc Williams knew and cared for everyone within Jefferson County and delivered generations of their babies. Molly, the bay mare drew his buggy while Rowdy, the hound, always rode in the seat next to him. Doc Williams was known for his love and compassion for animals as well as his human patients. From the earliest years of his practice he had worn out four buggies and five horses. Rowdy was the tenth of his mandatory buggy seat dogs.

"She's been asking for the two of you. I have other calls to make but I'll be back later to check in on her. Nice to see you back," he offered his hand to Rollie. "I just wish it could have been under happier circumstances." Rollie shook Doc Williams' hand but with a puzzled look.

"I've taken care of your family since you were just a baby," the doctor explained. " It's been a long time and you obviously don't remember me.... but I remember you. I'm sorry about your aunt. She's been a dear friend. I just wish there was more I could do... but there isn't." He turned and left the house with an air of profound sorrow.

Emilie and Rollie crept quietly into Aunt Durley's room and sat one on either side of the bed. She opened her eyes with effort and gave them a weak smile.

"My children," she said. Emilie clasped Durley's limp hand, raised it for a kiss and struggled to contain her tears. Rollie could only stare at his large, rough hands in his lap.

"Rollie," Aunt Durley begged weakly. "Rollie, I'm leaving you soon. I'm the only one left. Do you want to know or not?"

He hesitated only a moment. "Yes, Ma'am. I cain't find the peace without it. I reckon I'm finally ready. Please tell us if'n you feel up to it."

Mary Emma's second child was not due for another three months when Paul suddenly died. One moment Paul was laughing and the next moment clutching his chest. His long legs simply folded beneath him and he hit the floor dead. Little Rollie, asleep upstairs heard his mother's scream and then the wailing commenced. The sound of it cut through his head like a knife. The hair on his neck stood up and crinkled against the skin. He clamped fists over his ears to shut out the sound but it seemed to go on forever. Eventually he could hear voices downstairs as the hired hand arrived and then left again to fetch Doc Williams from town. The little boy hid in his room, forgotten until the next morning when Aunt Durley arrived and took him back to the trading post and to the care of his sweet Grand-mere.

They buried Paul in the peach orchard and marked his grave with a simple wooden cross. Mary Emma, unable to even acknowledge her son, much less care for him asked her mother and sister to take him for a while. In a matter of days, disaster visited her again when the hired hand plundered the house, stole the last of her money and fled the area.

Mary Emma would have thought it not possible to experience such pain and still be able to survive. She simply lay down and let it roll over and crush her. If she could have willed herself to die, it would have been a relief to do so. In her entire life she had never even slept in a room alone much less an entire empty house. Raised and protected by a strong father, loved and nurtured by a gentle mother, she and her older sister, Durley, had little experience with surviving in a hostile world. After their marriage, Paul took the place of her parents and provided her with an existence free from any concern beyond caring for their home and immediate family life. She was incapable of standing up as an individual and taking charge of her life. Emotionally crippled, she had become the severed half of a pair.

Durley begged Mary Emma to stay with them at the trading post until after the baby was born. Within days of Mary Emma's arrival she received a visitor in the guise of a concerned official. Local Judge Rufus Coble, a stocky, big boned man with dapper clothes and impeccable manners came to offer his services to the grieving widow. With an eagle-like hooked nose, olive skin, piercing black eyes and dark slicked back hair, he immediately put Durley in mind of a bird of prey. Rufus arranged for a young couple to live in the old cabin on the farm, and act as caretakers until her return. Charming, solicitous and sympathetic, he easily convinced Mary Emma to delegate the handling of Paul's estate and all of her concerns to him. He brought small gifts to the family and courted little Rollie's friendship. Outraged, Durley argued with her sister over the man's intrusion while their gentle mother, unable to cope beyond care of the child, began a slow retreat to a safer place in her mind. Durley was alone and helpless with her trepidations while the Judge steadily advanced his agenda with flowers and subtle attentions to the grieving widow. Mary Emma fell easy prey and soon grew to rely on his administration of her farm and personal well-being. Her gratitude for his assistance became muddled with feelings of love and dependence.

Six weeks after the birth of her second son, Curtis, Mary Emma wed Judge Rufus Coble and they all moved back to her farm as a family. In the beginning he treated Rollie with kindness, especially in front of the woman. At the same time he gradually assumed control of the farm and everything on it. The first to go was the fine freight wagon and patent leather harnesses with the brass trim. Plow mules did not need such finery he declared and they were quite lucky that his brother just happened to be in need of such a rig. He did them a great favor. Next to go were Paul's tools, knife collection and gold watch. The money was needed for next year's crops. Again, they were lucky he knew someone to take these unnecessary items off their hands. Mary Emma said nothing while Rollie, old enough to understand the outrage and transgression, was still too young to stop it. His resentment grew with every day that Rufus slept under his father's roof. One day he entered the house just as the man was preparing to leave. Rufus carried the rifle that Gerd Hessler used that long ago day defending the St. Louis Arsenal. Paul cherished the weapon and the memory of the brave friend who had entrusted it to his care.

"That's my Papa's gun." Rollie declared indignantly.

Rufus eyed the red-faced youngster who stood defiantly in his path. Part of him found it amusing and the other part felt anger that the child would dare to challenge him.

"Of course it is your father's gun," he answered through a malevolent smile. "Guns do not belong in a house where little children live. That's why I am putting it in a safe place until you and Curtis are older." He pushed past the boy and strode stiff legged out the door.

From that day an undeclared war commenced. The more Rollie opposed Rufus, the further his mother withdrew. Her world revolved around baby Curtis while outsiders overran her home and business. Durley visited with Mary Emma and the children every Sunday. Her sister's nervousness, withdrawal and occasional teary eyes were of a great concern. On more than one occasion she noted bruises on Mary Emma's arms and face. The explanation always involved a fall or accidental bump.

An inevitable clash between Rufus and Red River came on the day when his own riding horse went lame and he decided to try out the mustang. When Rufus attempted to saddle the nervous animal, Red River shied and began plunging violently. Livid with anger, he cursed the horse and tied him to a post in the barn, then strode out to find his whip. Rollie, who had been watching the whole occurrence, untied Red River, removed his halter and lead rope and scurried to a dark corner to hide.

Rufus, a long buggy whip in his hand, threw open the barn door and for a moment stood face to face with the wild-eyed horse. The next instant he looked up into a sea of black, then flipped over to the ground where his face impacted the dirt.

Red River had bolted directly into and over the violent man, never stopping until he reached open meadows and freedom.

Oooooh, I'm in fer it now, the little boy thought. His pounding heart felt as if it were in his throat and he found it difficult to even breathe. Trying to become invisible, he pulled his head down and shrank into a tight ball against the wall.

"Rollie, Rollie," Rufus called sweetly. "I know you're here. I just want to talk to you. Come on out now." His heavy boots clomped feet away from Rollie's hiding place but in the dim light he was unable to see the child. Trembling with fear Rollie waited for eternal tense moments until the man finally left the barn, closing the big creaking door behind him. Hours passed and it seemed that the supper hour must have been getting close. He hoped that Rufus had been diverted to something else and would be cooled off by now. He crawled on hands and knees from his hiding place into the dimming light. All seemed quiet. Easing over to the door, he tried to open it just enough to slip out, but it creaked so loud his heart pounded again. Within two steps into the barnyard, the big man pounced, grabbing the back of his neck in a crushing grip.

"You little bastard! Thought you were pretty smart didn't ya. We'll see how smart you are in a minute." He yanked the child roughly by the arm, dragging him back into the darkening barn and slung him mightily across a stall. Rollie slammed into the back wall and lay stunned. Rufus slammed the stall door shut, and began pummeling the crouching boy with his fists and heavy boots. Rollie raised an arm across his face to ward off the first kick and the bone cracked with a sickening sound. The following blows were never felt. His mind blocked the reality and another part of him seemed to be watching it happen from a distant place.

Breathless from his frenzy Rufus drew back, his arms hanging loosely by his sides. "Now you little bastard," he hissed. "Get your sorry ass back up to the house an tell your Ma the horse threw you. Tell her that he ran away." Poking his finger roughly against the boys bleeding nose, he threatened, "You ever tell her any different I'll kill you deader than hell myself. You got it?"

102

The terrified boy bobbed his head yes, whereupon Rufus grabbed the injured arm and jerked him to his feet. Rollie shrieked in pain and was rewarded with a slap to the back of his head.

Without a word, his dispassionate mother had cleaned the wounds and tucked him into bed. When Rollie finally heard the old clock downstairs bonging out the midnight hour, he rolled onto his side and stood erect, every part of his body in agony. Pulling on his clothes and boots, he wrapped a blanket, shawl style, around his shoulders and snuck out of the house. Once clear of the yard he ran down the road as fast as his protesting body could go. More than once he dived into the underbrush beside the road when he imagined the sound of a pursuer. The eastern sky just started to lighten when he finally made it to his Gran-mére's Antonia trading post and fell across the doorway semi conscious.

He fell into a swirling, smoky place where people hovered over his prone body. He remembered Gran-mére, Aunt Durley, Doc Williams, and later on, several strange men who simply stared at him and than left the room. Yes, he especially remembered the men because they seemed angry and wondered if they had come to punish him again.

18 *SECRETS AND SINS*

Two nights after Rollie ran away, Rufus prepared for bed. Mary Emma and the baby were already asleep and he was ready to go up and join them when he heard the sound of horses in the yard. Glancing at the front window, lights flickered as if from a fire. Flinging the front door open he was shocked to be confronted with a circle of horsemen carrying flaming torches. Through wide eyes and a gaping mouth he could only stare in shock, for all of the men were disguised with hoods and long robes.

"What do you want?" he stammered.

A rope with slip noose hissed out and over his head in reply. The horseman who threw the rope quickly looped it around the saddle horn and pulled back sharply on the reins. The noose tightened where it had come to rest, across one shoulder and under the opposite arm. He was dragged roughly off of the porch and fell heavily into the yard. Another rider prodded his horse next to the downed man.

"On your feet an git on that horse," he commanded.

A third rider led the horse he was to mount. Once in the saddle, they circled around him and all galloped into the darkness.

No one ever really knew what happened to Rufus Coble in the woods that night. The farm hand found him laying in the yard just before dawn the next day; his body covered with bruises, welts and dried blood. They went to the creek where he allowed the hand to help him wash away the blood and brought him clean, dry clothes to hide the marks. Not too many days afterward, Rufus announced that he had found God and was going to become a preacher. He spent countless hours studying the good book, preparing lessons and sermons for all the hapless souls who had the misfortune of meeting him.

For the next year, Durley continued her weekly visits to Mary Emma and baby Curtis. The child, happy and plump, toddled about the house, babbling and busy. Mary Emma, too, seemed more content but never asked about Rollie. Durley surmised that would open a door to the place Mary Emma did not want to go. On the rare occasion that she saw Rufus, he was pleasant but distant. She could not help notice he walked with a funny twisted gait and was never without long sleeves even on the hottest of days.

One Sunday afternoon, Durley hugged her sister and nephew good-by, then strode across the yard to her buggy. Rufus spied her and crossed over to the buggy for a word.

"Leaving so soon, Durley? I was hoping to have a word with you today."

"Really?" And what would that be about?" she asked, barely able to disguise her hatred.

"Have you been saved, Durley?"

"WHAT?"

"I said have you been saved?"

"What right do you, *of all people*, have to ask me such a question?" she demanded, her anger barely under control.

"Durley. Calm down just a minute. I'm here to tell you that I'm not the man you once thought I was. I've become a Christian and I've been called to spread the gospel and God's word. Praise God."

Durley seethed. "You dammed hypocrite! Many more Christians like you un the devil'd be out of work!" she spat. Wheeling about in a fury, she pulled herself up into the buggy, flicked the horse's back with the whip and drove out in a swirl of dust.

Several more months had passed when, early one morning, Doc Williams pounded on the trading post door and shouted for them to wake up. When Durley finally came to the door, he grabbed her hand.

"Quick Durley, get dressed and come with me to the farm. I just got word there's been an accident and they've sent for me. You'd best come along."

On arrival at the farm, the hired hand waited in the yard for the doctor and pointed toward the second story of the house. They ran inside and up the stairs to find Mary Emma sitting on the floor in Curtis' room. She clutched the toddler tightly to her bosom, rocking and humming to him. Doc Williams approached cautiously and crouched down next to her.

"Let me see the baby," he instructed quietly. Mary Emma looked at him with glazed, bewildered eyes. Gently he pulled her arms away and took the baby from her. The small, breathless body hung limp in his arms. Removing the boy's clothes, he found ugly welts on the trunk; a large bloody knot on the side of the head and the left eye was swollen shut. The right eye stared to infinity.

Mary Emma looked from one to the other of them in tearful despair. "He fell down the stairs, he fell down the stairs," she repeated over and over.

Durley and the doctor looked to each other unbelieving that this could happen. At that very moment Durley's fury was to the extreme that she could not even react. Every part of her being turned to icy coldness. Doc Williams wrapped the baby in a blanket, placed him back in his mother's arms and led her down the stairs and into his buggy. When they drove out of the yard, Rufus Coble was nowhere to be seen.

Baby Curtis was buried in the peach orchard next to his father, Paul Burroughs. The death had been reported to the local constable who regretfully objected that nothing could be done for lack of a witness. The death was ruled accidental. Rollie reluctantly agreed to attend the graveside service. It would be the first time that he had seen his mother or stepfather since coming to live with Aunt Durley. He endured his mother's outstretched arms and tearful hug, but simply refused to even look at Rufus. The town's local minister provided the service but near the conclusion, Rufus stepped forward with a bible in his hand.

"I'd like to say a word over my boy," he said piously.

"DON'T," Mary Emma cried out. Then in a subdued tone, "...please don't."

Catching Durley's steely glare from across the casket, Rufus looked momentarily stunned, then conceded politely, bowed his head and took a step backward.

As the service concluded, all their friends and neighbors offered condolences and began leaving the farm. Young Rollie listened to the subdued crying of his relatives as they said their last goodbye to Curtis. In the end, his mother's quiet cries gave way to the hideous wailing that he heard the night of his father's death. Intense anger fell over him like a red veil. He felt neither sympathy nor sorrow. Too young and traumatized to deal with so many conflicting emotions, he simply bolted and ran toward home. Arriving at the trading post out of breath, his clothing disheveled, he flew up to the third floor. Hunkering down in a dark corner the child cried out his own pain in private. Any feelings for his mother before this day had been void, but what he felt for her now was pure disdain.

What Durley felt for her sister was more in the line of disgust. But Rufus...the feeling for Rufus was burning hatred. For a week after the funeral her mind churned with violent, evil thoughts. At night she lay awake staring into the darkness and thinking of what to do. This evil man could not be allowed to escape punishment for his crimes. If not for herself or her sister, she owed it to her secret love Paul and his two sons who had suffered at the hands of this brute. Finally on the eighth day after the funeral Durley sighted the handyman passing through the town with baby pigs and chickens for market. Mary Emma and Rufus would be alone on the farm. She waited until her mother and nephew slept, then dressed in her father's pants and shirt and crept stealthily from the post. Stored in the horse shed, the buggy had been prepared earlier in the day and contained all that she would need for her night's work. She had only to hitch the horse to it and get out of the lot without being heard. Every bump and turn in the road was memorized from the countless trips to visit her sister. About one eighth of a mile from the front gate, a side trail veered off into the woods. It narrowed down to a walking trail blocked with underbrush. After struggling to get the horse and buggy backed into the little trail out of sight, she unloaded her equipment and struck out to the farm on foot. Her pocket was filled with matches and a striker to light them with. In the left hand she carried a metal can of kerosene and in the right hand, her father's loaded 12-gauge shotgun.

The house stood dark and silent. Without warning the yard dog charged, barking ferociously, but stopped as suddenly with recognition. With a pounding heart and short of breath, Durley had to rest for a minute to recover. The dog whined and nuzzled at her hand to be petted but her attention was riveted on a woodshed that stood to the backside of the house. The shed stood in clear view of the bedroom window where the couple slept. Brushing the dog aside she ran across the yard, ducked into the shed and splashed kerosene on the walls and contents within. When finished, she backed out the door, threw the empty can back inside and took a deep breath.

Durley felt faint, her heart pounded so. The fact that she had committed to such violence was unbelievable. For a brief moment her resolve weakened, but only until she recalled the reasons for being there.

"Rollie and Curtis. Rollie and Curtis." she whispered over and over to herself for courage. Taking a deep breath, she took another step back, lit a small torch with trembling hands and threw it into the shed. The fire exploded with a loud roar and flames shot into the sky as high as the nearby treetops. The dog ran wildly about the yard barking hysterically. Within minutes, a light was struck in the house. Rufus, barefoot and clad only in his pants and undershirt, burst out the back door and ran into the yard. Stopping in front of the shed, his head jerked from left to right as he looked for anything nearby to fight the fire with. The sight of him turned Durley icy cold and she strode up behind him strong and sure.

"Rufus. Rufus Coble," she called out. Rufus whirled about and faced her.

"Durley, what the hell you doing here? What's going on?" His voice trailed off as he saw her raise Oscar's shotgun. Durley pointed it at his face…. and pulled the trigger.

19 *LOOSE ENDS*

Weaver watched the man ambling toward him. Head lowered under the wide-brimmed hat, he walked with a heavy, aimless step. Thoughtlessly he patted the mule on the nose, "Hey Weaver," and waited for his Palouse horse, Hon-ga, to join them. Since the day of their big confrontation in the pen, the two animals had become close pals. Weaver looked to the horse with, almost, adoring eyes and followed him about. Emilie remarked that she almost thought the mule sometimes looked to Rollie with the same maudlin expression.

Rollie's heart felt almost as heavy as his feet today. Since Aunt Durley's death the previous week, he and Emilie had simply whiled away the days, unable to pick a direction or hold a thought. Assuming his familiar thinking stance at the fence, he leaned his head against the top rail and his arms and elbows braced on the next rail. Staring at Hon-ga, a wave of intense homesickness flowed through him and his thoughts turned to the Clyatt ranch that had been home for so many years. He thought of the Clyatt family, Delmar, Miz Sophie, Shelby, his best friend Purdy, the Nez Perce Indians, Matthew, little Daniel, Two Feathers and Mary. Then he wondered about Cecelia Gideon and if she was still working for Miz Suzy Jane. The thought of Cecelia in addition to everything else that had happened finally brought a tear. Angrily he wiped it away and determined it best that he finish things up here and head home. He'd found out what he came for and it was time to get back to whatever lay ahead.

Emilie looked resigned when he gave her the news.

"I figured you'd be wanting to leave soon and I kind of prepared myself for it."

"I recall ya tellin me about a gentleman in St. Louis that ya were kind of sweet on. Do ya want me to take ya there an find him afore I git back on that train?" Rollie raised his eyebrows in a questioning look.

"I've already written a letter to him but haven't posted it as yet. I've lived here in this trading post my entire life. If I continue to stay here, I'll never know what else there is out in the world, but if I go…honestly, Rollie, I'm not sure about what I want right now. I've heard it said that if you're not sure what to do, than don't do anything. Sooner or later I'll know what's right. I feel such an attachment to this old place and the history that it represents…but then you think about that dreadful story that Aunt Durley left us with. I still just can't believe it. To think, that all these years she has carried that around inside her. But we still don't know what happened after that night and whatever happened to our mother."

Rollie pondered about it for a moment and then offered, "Let's go call on Doc Williams. I have a feelin he'll have the answers."

The pair walked the dusty road into the settlement and to Doc Williams's little frame house off the main street. His wife, Patrice, showed them into the doctor's waiting area and informed them he was out on calls but expected back soon.

"He's out riding around somewhere with his horse and dog. Some folks are getting those new machines to drive around but that'll never happen here," she laughed. "I can't really blame him though. Old Molly knows exactly where to go and just between us, he says, "Home Molly," and then takes a nap while she gets him there. Half the time, I think some of those patients could be coming here to the office but he worries so about them, he wouldn't have it any other way." She left the room smiling to herself.

"I think she wouldn't have it any other way either," Emilie whispered kindly."

Noon arrived with Rollie's stomach growling and he glimpsed, embarrassedly at Emilie. She laughed and rubbed her own stomach with empathy. "Do you want to come back later?"

"No. This is sumthin that we need to do. It's been too long now."

She nodded agreement and they were rewarded a short time later when the doctor's buggy drove up the street. Rowdy sitting tall in the seat, next to his master, projected an air of importance for his position.

As soon as Patrice informed the doctor of their presence, he waved them into the office and gestured at a pair of chairs aligned next to his massive roll top desk. Rowdy followed them inside and lay on a rug at the doctor's feet. Folding his hands, he looked from one to the other over the top of wire spectacles.

"I figured you two would come around sooner or later. She told you, didn't she?"

They looked to one another, a little panicked. What was it that the doctor thought Aunt Durley had told them? How much did he know about Rufus' shooting that night? Cautiously, Emilie began.

"Doc Williams, we know that Rufus probably killed our brother, Curtis. We also know that someone shot and killed him the night of the fire out at the farm. My mother must have been expecting me when he died, because my birthday was five months later. What we don't know is what became of our mother after that...or what about the farm?"

She looked to Rollie with a question in her eyes. Catching her gist, he leaned forward a little enthused, "an I jest cain't seem to recall where I wuz when all this happened. I've tried an tried but nothing comes to me bout any of this. We wuz kind of hoping since ya've known the whole family fer all these years that ya kin put it all to rest fer us."

The doctor leaned back in the chair, lowered his head thoughtfully and pressed his fingers to pursed lips. Finally, after a moment's silence he began.

"To what you are both wondering, the answer is yes. I know that Durley Yeager shot and killed Rufus Coble. She drove out to the farm alone that night and lit the fire that brought him out into the open. As a matter of fact, everyone in town figured that she was the one that had done it, even the sheriff. The fact is, that man was such a mean son-of-a-bitch that we all were glad she did it. Scuse my language Emilie. The sheriff declared his death was at the hand of an unknown assailant or assailants. The matter was never brought up again. Now about your mother…she was indeed expecting when this happened and she moved back to the trading post with your aunt. Your aunt ran down to get me the night you were born. I delivered you up in that front, second story bedroom. As for you, Rollie, I recall your aunt talking about how angry you had become. Seems you blamed your mother for a lot of what happened and wouldn't come around her. In fact, she wasn't there at the post for long at all when you just up and ran away. No one knew anything about you, whether you were alive or dead, sick or well, happy or sad, until you just showed back up here a few weeks ago. Durley was sick for a long, long time but I always knew in my heart that she was holding on for you Rollie. Some part of you must have felt it too, because you got here just in time. I believe she was at peace when she died. You claim you can't remember any of this. That is not surprising to me. You were just a lad when ole Rufus almost beat you to death and then did the same to Curtis. He beat up on your mother too, but she was too weak to stand up and throw his worthless ass out. That's probably a lot of why you were so mad with her…. that it had to cost Curtis's life before somebody stopped him. I think, Rollie, that in time you will start to put faces to the stories that you've been told. It will come back and I predict a full recovery for you," he smiled gently.

"What about mother?" Emilie persisted.

"I guess she had a hard time living with everything that happened too. Not long after you were born, Emilie, she met up with some fellow passing through on a riverboat and left with him. She sent word back that she was in New Orleans. One day your aunt got a letter from some attorney giving her papers for the farm and custody of both you children. Your mother was as weak as her sister, Durley, was strong. She always ran away when things got tough."

"Do you mean to tell me that Aunt Durley still owns the farm?" Emilie asked hopefully.

"No, No. She sold it right away and that's about all that I can tell you."

"Oh," she murmured with great disappointment.

The couple thanked the doctor profusely, bade him goodbye and were halfway out the door when Rollie thought of something else.

"Oh, Doc Williams. Do ya have any idea of what happened to that pair of big mules that my pa had? I kind of remember them an the black mustang too."

The old doctor rubbed his chin and thought about it. Finally, he answered.

"As I recall, your aunt had those mules brought in to the Higgins' farm and paid those folks to take care of them. I think they finally just both died of old age out in that big south pasture. She was kind of sentimental that way. As for Red River, he was a legend around here – like a ghost horse. He hung around but nobody could ever catch him and then finally he just disappeared. I figure he must have been pretty old by then as well, so he probably went off and died too." He smiled indulgently as they thanked him again and started home to ponder all they had learned.

No sooner than they had turned the corner onto Main Street, another elderly gentleman raised his arm in greeting.

"Miss Emilie. Miss Emilie. Please wait." Pudgy and balding, long thinning hair was combed sideward over his shiny, pink dome. Rollie gave the man a quick up, down scan and found himself impressed with the fine gray suit, plaid vest and the heavy gold watch chain that draped across his rounded middle. Another quick glimpse at his sister's face betrayed her amusement. Her amused expression was not blatant nor even mildly rude. Rollie had just come to know her well enough to read beyond her first expressions. He found himself looking forward to the conversation waiting for when they were alone again.

"Ah, Miss Emilie," he reached for her hand and brushed it lightly with his lips, "...and this must be your big brother that I have been hearing about." He smiled broadly in greeting to Rollie.

"How do you do Mr. Sinclair. Yes, this is my brother Rollie Burroughs. Rollie, this is Mr. Sinclair…Aunt Durley's banker."

Revelation of the man's profession raised some mild interest along with Rollie's left eyebrow.

"Howdy, Mr. Sinclair," he offered along with his extended hand. "Pleased to meet ya."

"Entirely my honor, Sir. Our meeting this fine day is most auspicious. I am expected back in my office as we speak. Do you both have time to accompany me so that we can discuss something of a private nature?"

Rollie bemoaned his complaining stomach but the man's invitation peaked his curiosity.

"I'm sorry Mr. Sinclair, but exactly what is your business an where is your office?" Mr. Sinclair looked momentarily puzzled.

"Oh I am so sorry Mr. Burroughs. I am the President of the Antonia State Farmer's Bank. Your aunt was one of my very good customers as well as a dear friend."

Again, that flick of amusement sparked across Emilie's face. An exchanged look of questioning passed between the brother and sister. Rollie shrugged his shoulders and answered for them both.

"Why not?"

Once settled into the banker's office, Rollie began to feel amused as well. Mr. Sinclair's heavy oak desk and brown leather office chair dwarfed the short man. Momentarily forgetting himself, he plopped back in the chair, his arms draped loosely on the chair arms and his shinny black shoes barely brushed the floor. He reminded Rollie of a small child playing grown up. Rollie quickly looked away as Mr. Sinclair scooted forward so that his feet rested flat on the floor. He dared not look at his sister for he was beginning to feel her emotion. Rude, spontaneous giggling lay just below the surface testing their manners and self-control.

"Your dear aunt appointed me executor of her estate some years ago. I am most proud and honored to report that she also entrusted me to invest and oversee a certain sum of capital realized from the sale of your mother's farm." The little man obviously gloried in his own self-importance as he dangled the information like bait. Their amusement with his pretentious manners was quickly forgotten at this surprising revelation.

"You will be most gratified to know that under my guardianship and control, the farm proceeds have grown to a significant amount. It was her intention that because of my comprehensive and significant background in investment banking..."

Rollie's eyes narrowed in irritation as the pompous little man monopolized the conversation, dramatizing and dragging out the conclusion for the sake of his own ego.

"Mr. Sinclair." he finally interrupted testily, stood up and leaned across the desk irritably. "Me an my sister are both purty hungry an wantin to git home. Kin we jest get to the point here...please?"

Mr. Sinclair seemingly shrank in size as the red-faced cowboy puffed up larger than he already was. Quickly he rummaged through a stack of papers on the corner of the imposing desk and drew out a ledger sheet. Laying it on the desk in front of them, he began pointing to entries and explaining the individual columns and figures. When he finally pointed to the final figure, Emilie gasped and covered the bottom of her face with both hands. Rollie's eyes grew large and round as he took a step backward and plopped down into his chair. Neither of them had ever imagined having more than a few dollars at any one time. Not only did they now have a significant amount of money to share there was also the trading post property.

Having disarmed the aggressive cowboy, Mr. Sinclair once again assumed control of the meeting. At it's conclusion the shaken, dazed pair left the banker's office and headed to Daisy's Café for a much-delayed meal.

"I reckon I'm in a position where I kin afford to treat my baby sister to lunch," Rollie joked. "I jest wish it was sum place grand so we could really celebrate. I jest can't believe any of this."

"Me neither," Emilie's head rocked back and forth in denial.   In less than one day's time, our entire lives are different. I don't know how to deal with all of this - - or know what to do with myself now."

20 *THOUGHTS OF HOME*

Hon-ga stepped out with a quick, light pace. Catching his spirit of enthusiasm, Weaver followed closely. The heavy, dark mood hovering over Hon-ga's rider didn't descend to their level. Rollie's mixed emotion about leaving was best described by Emilie who called it a double-edged sword. A melancholy that started to grip him, even before Aunt Durley's death, now gnawed at his being. Thoughts of his Idaho home, the people and the animals there plagued him. He missed the Saturday shopping trips to town with Miz Sophie and raucous times at Miz Suzy Jane's tavern with friend Purdy Roxlo. Ranch owner, Delmar Clyatt, Miz Sophie's husband, had entrusted his entire family, livestock and property to Rollie. Thinking back on that trust, Rollie realized how much he had taken his position and responsibilities for granted. Shelby Clyatt, their young son, lived in the East with his grandparents while the couple established the ranch and prepared a better life for him. The boy finally arrived, shy and introverted, but educated and intelligent. Under the tutelage of Rollie, Purdy and their Nez Perce co-worker, Matthew, the boy blossomed into a gregarious, mischievous, earthy individual worthy of his mentors.

Thoughts of little Daniel almost brought tears. Rollie longed to hold the little boy in front of his big saddle again and ride out to check the cows and horses. Even Matthew had a place in Rollie's longing. Adversaries yes, but an underlying friendship and respect over shadowed any past conflicts. Yes, Rollie thought to himself with half a smile. I even miss my little rat-faced, runty friend, Matthew. How many times had he tormented Matthew with name-calling and taunts? Sometimes it was rough, good-natured fun and other times not so good-natured. It was all the same to Matthew. He usually ignored Rollie and went about his quiet way. What I wouldn't have given to have parents like him, to have his childhood with all the love and support that Two Feathers and Mary gave, he thought. With the Palouse horses that Matthew raised, his life was filled with a passion and a purpose. Yet another thing missing from Rollie's life – passion and purpose.

When his thoughts finally worked around to Cecelia, a hopeful idea accompanied them. With the money from his parent's estate, Rollie had something to offer the ambitious woman. Maybe a little ranch of their own, a proper house and even that sewing business in town that she aspired to.

I really need to get home he nagged himself. However, the other side of that double-edged sword was saying good-bye. He and Emilie had become very close. Never before could he remember feeling such a loving bond with another human. Sure, the early childhood memories of his mother and father were slowly surfacing. He could vaguely feel the remnants of warmth and love from that time but that's mostly all it was, just vague and far removed feelings. Aunt Durley had gained his love and gratitude in the short time they had together. Now he had to live with the regret of losing all those years with the one person who gave her all to protect and care for him.

As his old aunt lay dying, he clutched her hands, bent over the bed and whispered, "Thank you Aunt Durley. Thank you fer caring bout us an takin care of us. I love you too, Aunt Durley." His pain, so great, choked his voice and distorted the words. Slipping to a far away place, she still heard him though, for a single tear escaped from behind closed eyes and then she slept.

Emilie talked to her brother about one day moving west with him. Her whole life had centered on the trading post and their aunt. Now, for the first time, she was alone in the old, decaying, three-story building. The one man who had ever paid her any mind lived in St. Louis. A grain broker, he traveled between the farmers of rural Missouri to the exporters in New Orleans and back again. His usual mode of travel was by steamboat on the Mississippi with occasional side trips to the extended farming areas where he first met Emilie. Naïve and innocent she fell quickly for his smooth talk and sweet attention. Despite how much she thought she loved and wanted this man, her responsibility to Aunt Durley's well being took precedence. In the beginning he called on her frequently but in recent months she had heard nothing from him. He left her with promises of a new life with him in the city when she found herself free to leave. Rollie was smart enough to know that she had given herself completely to this traveling man. The thought of his sister being duped and used brought a cold, hard glint to his eye.

A letter addressed to the man lay on the desk for the past week. Trying to feel her out, Rollie gestured toward the envelope.

"Why ain't ya mailed that letter to yer friend yet?"

A look of distress passed fleetingly across her face and she squirmed in the chair.

"I guess I'm afraid of his response – or even if he will respond at all," she answered meekly. "I guess I can't get hurt if I don't send it. But then again, I have nothing at all if I just stay on here alone, do I? What kind of life is this?"

He rose slowly from the creaky, old cane bottomed chair, his eyes never leaving the envelope across the room. He walked to the desk, picked up the envelope and studied the name and address.

"Arley Hambach, Greater Missouri Mills and Grain Brokerage." Deep in thought, Rollie absent-mindedly tapped the envelope against the back of his free hand. "Is this the address where his business is?"

"Yes," she answered simply and shifted nervously in her chair again.

"Why is it goin to this business? Where does he live?" Rollie grilled.

"I don't know. He told me he moved around a lot and didn't want to give me an address for fear my letters would be lost." The moment she stated the feeble excuse aloud, she knew how ridiculous it sounded.

"I fear I've played the fool," her voice trembled. Humiliated and looking downward, she scrunched up her face to keep from crying in front of him.

Rollie fought back his anger. His sweet, gentle sister did not need to see that side of him.

"Tell you what I kin do," he started with a gentleness he did not feel. "I kin hand-carry this letter to this Arley fella an see where he stands. That way you don't hav ta face him if'n it's over tween ya. An if he does have feelins fer ya, I'll let ya know if I approve of im or not." He grinned lamely at his own attempt for a little humor. She recognized his effort, smiled slightly through misted eyes and agreed with an affirmative nod.

Safely tucked in a deep jacket pocket the letter traveled with him on this day. Before he left, Emilie also gave him Aunt Durley's secessionist's quilt, freshly laundered, carefully folded and packed in a bundle with his clean clothes. The very last thing she gave him was a handcrafted German rifle that had been found hidden away behind Durley's old walnut chiffonier.

"Oh, look Rollie." Emilie held the rifle, an expression of wonderment on her face. "Do you think this is your Father's gun - - - you know, the one that Rufus took?"

Rollie rose slowly from his chair, crossed the room and took it from her outstretched arms. To find and actually hold this unique weapon loosened a wave of emotion the like of which he had never experienced since. Clutching the rifle close to his chest, he actually felt the presence of his father, remembered the image of his face, how he smiled and how he walked and how he talked. Rollie's legs weakened beneath him and it felt as if the breath was being mashed from his body. Embarrassed, he turned away from Emilie and took the rifle near the light of the window, pretending to examine it. Once a gleaming blue-black steel with highly polished wooden stock, it was now covered with scratches and dull from years of neglect. Elaborate hand engraved metal lay beneath flakes of rust. Big rough hands caressed the weapon as he silently determined to bring it back to its full glory.

Smiling to herself, Emilie respectfully left the room.

21 *FAREWELL MISSOURI*

Nearing the city Rollie slowed the pace and looked for a place to camp. Better to enter the city with a full day ahead lest he lose his way. Roaming unfamiliar streets after dark did not appeal to him.

Breaking through a stand of Hawthorn trees and River Birch, he came upon a sloping meadow near the river. Trumpet creeper vine covered the lower bushes and trees. Bright sunlight still streamed through, inviting brightly colored hummingbirds to the vine. Clusters of Indian Paintbrush with bright red flowers, intermingled with white prairie clover spread outward to borders of white and violet Iris that grew closer to the waters edge. The color and beauty of so many flowers gave him a feeling of peace and the wish that he could share the splendor with Emilie.

Hon-ga and Weaver benefited Rollie's improved mood by way of a hearty rub down each. He then staked them out on long ropes amid the lush meadow grass and prepared his spot for the night. While campfire coffee made from Mississippi river water simmered, he wolfed the last of Emilie's homemade bread, pickles and cheese. Good thing this is the last night out he mused and slurped in a big slug of the hot coffee.

"Eiyee," he grimaced with a hard swallow. The horse and mule both lifted their heads and looked with mild interest in his direction. "Dang!" he spat. "River tastes like shit," he offered to them as explanation. Bemused with himself then, he leaned back and chuckled. "Talkin to a horse and a dumb mule. Good thing I'll be back with people come mornin."

If Rollie Burroughs had been unable to remember his early life before, he did not have a problem now. With every new day, his head crammed with fresh memories, both good and bad. Atop that, dreams of a new life on his own ranch, with a home and maybe even a wife and children swirled and mixed in the flow. At night, even when sleep came, his mind would not turn off for all the new information and occurrences of the past few months. I have to slow this thing down and take time to get over it he scolded himself. Fer sure, it's goin to take awhile to adjust ta it all. No sooner had he thought the words, then a vision of the black mustang, Red River, dashed into his head and brought a sad little smile.

Addressing the grazing animals he announced, "When we git back home, I'm gonna christen that crazy black mustang we got. He's gonna be Red River the second."

With a satisfied sign, he lay back, folded his calloused hands upon his chest and gazed out into the emerging star filled night. Tomorrow's business in the city, he reminded himself. This other stuffs got to wait.

Mid morning found Rollie and his four footed comrades searching up and down bricked streets for the office of Greater Missouri Mills and Grain Brokerage. A corner newspaper boy directed him to the address on Finney Avenue. Expecting to find a warehouse with silo or other storage facilities, he was very surprised to find a small, shabby storefront office with the business name painted across the door. Sitting astride the heavy Palouse horse, he shook his head sadly and pressed a grubby hand against his eyes.

"Hon-ga, old buddy, I'm skeered ta even go in there – cause I already know what I'm goin to find out." Leaning forward, he swung a leg across the saddle and stepped down, his eyes never leaving the storefront. He tied Hon-ga and Weaver to a front post, removed his hat and walked into the darkened office. A plump, matronly woman sat on a high stool behind the counter, poring over a stack of papers. Clad in a limp white blouse, with a black ribbon tie, she looked up at him through dark circled eyes and brushed a wisp of messy brown hair from her brow.

"Can I help you," she asked in a flat voice.

"Yes'um. I'm looking fer Mr. Hambeck. Is this his business place?"

122

"It is, but he's not here right now. I expect him anytime though. Do you have business with him?"

"Yes'um. I do. Reckon, I'll jest wait outside on the stoop till he gits here."

"Well, I'm Mrs. Hambeck. I don't usually work here in the office, but I can help if you'd like. Do you have grain to sell?"

Rollie flushed red, a wave of heat rolling across his face, his body and his brain.

"Yere, Mrs. Hambeck? Is yer husband the same grain broker that travels up un down the Mississippi to New Orleans selling farm goods?"

"Yes, he is. You've come to the right place. If you're not here to sell your crop, are you here to purchase?"

Rollie swallowed hard to conceal the scalding rage that he felt.

"No ma'am. It's neither. Me an your husband have common friends down river un I jest stopped to pay my respects un deliver a message. I ain't really met Mr. Hambeck personal yet. You two been married long?"

A weak smile crossed her lips and she nodded her head slightly. "Yes, we have. It will be 15 years next month, in fact."

"Really. That's right nice. How many young'uns you un your mister got?" he inquired sweetly.

"Three… two boys and a girl. Oh! Here comes my husband now." She looked past Rollie and through the window at a tall, slim, dapper dressed man crossing the street. He wore a professional gray business suit, high collared white shirt and black derby hat. Rollie's swift impression was that of a slick salesman capable of easily fooling a naïve, country girl like Emilie.

Rollie jumped to his feet and rushed to the door. "I'll jest meet with him outside here Ma'am. It was nice talking with ya." Rollie stepped out the door and with strong steps met the man near the edge of the street.

"Arley Hambeck?"

"Yes, I'm Arley Hambeck – and whom do I have the pleasure of talking with here?"

"Name's Burroughs. Rollie Burroughs. Mind stepping over beside the building here so's we kin have a word?"

"Why yes, yes of course," Arley responded hesitantly. He moved to the shaded side of the wooden office building and rubbing his hands together, leaned slightly forward.

"What's this about Mr. Burroughs? I assume you are here on business. Do you have crops to sell?"

"Not exactly. Ya see, I jest come from down Antonia way."

Arley's eyes widened slightly with the statement. Rollie continued with a deceptive, confidential tone.

"I met this lady there that I kind of had a hankerin fer but she says no. She's waiting on this gentleman from St. Louis who's comin to marry her an take her to live in the city."

Arley's face blanched white and he glanced nervously beyond Rollie's shoulder at the office window.

"Rollie waved a hand. "Naw, I didn't tell yere wife in yonder. An yep! I know about your three young'uns you got with her too," he smiled conspiratorially at the nervous man. "I jest want to know where things stand tween ya afore I take this any further. I don't want to mess in yere territory if'n ya understand what I mean here," he smiled devilishly at Arley.

Arley threw his head back with a dirty little laugh.

"That's very considerate of you Mr., Mr. ---"

"Burroughs. Name's Burroughs," Rollie offered.

"Yes, of course. That's very considerate of you Mr. Burroughs. I have no further interest in the lady. Since you mentioned Antonia, I assume you're talking about Emilie Coble."

Rollie nodded assent and raised his eyebrows in question for Arley to continue.

"You seem like a worldly fellow Mr. Burroughs and I'm sure you know how it is. Emilie is a nice girl ---clean, sweet, but really not too smart. They start getting serious, I just move on. Any port in a storm as they say." He grinned devilishly.

Rollie's rage burst with the speed and ferocity of a springing panther. Strong hard hands struck and grabbed the front of Arley's lapels. He snatched the man off of his feet and slung him toward the side of the building throwing him mightily against the frame wall.

"You som-bitch," he shrieked at the terrified man. With feet dangling above the ground, Arley's eyes bulged, his mouth worked wordlessly as he clutched madly at Rollie's massive hands. Blinking back tears of rage, Rollie drew backward and then smashed his forehead into Arley's face. Cartilage and bone crunched with a sickening thud beneath the blow. Blood gushed from his smashed nose and mouth. Rollie released his grip and the limp man crumpled into the dirt.

"Emilie Coble is my baby sister!" he spat at the body on the ground. She don't deserve to be treated like some whore an tossed away after." Rollie's body heaved up and down as he gulped in the air, his arms hanging limply at his sides. Arley lay curled in a ball, sobbing. Finally composing himself, Rollie sucked in a deep breath, leaned over the man and shook a finger in his face.

"Next time you travel down river, you make sure you give Antonia a wide range. Cause you ever-set foot there again, I'll know, an you're dead meat jest as sure as I'm a-standing here. Fact is, I'm gonna tell Emilie you are dead! Jest make sure she don't ever find out otherwise."

He spun about, stalked stiff-legged to his animals, mounted and headed back the way he'd come without a backward glance.

By the time Rollie reached Ryan's Stable near the old fairgrounds, his breathing was back to normal and he was actually feeling quite self-satisfied. A bruised, aching forehead proved to be the only blight to the incident. He dismounted stiffly, tied Hon-ga and Weaver to a rail outside the stable and wandered into the darkened building.

"Hello, hello…anybody home?" he called. Must be out at the track he mused. The wooden door to the Ryan's upstairs apartment creaked open and Meggie stepped out on the landing.

"Who's there?" she called.

"It's me, Miz Meggie. Rollie Burroughs."

"Oh my goodness!" she clapped her hands in joy. "Rollie. Come up. Please come up. Sonny just went down to the track for a minute. He'll be right back."

Leaving the door ajar for him, she rushed back inside and put a kettle of water on the stove for tea. Sonny found them on his return, sitting at the dinning room table enjoying the hot tea and some of his wife's ever-present sweet cakes. After a happy exchange of small talk, Sonny helped Rollie tend to his animals and together they polished off the last of the stable chores for the day.

Meggie happily prepared a company dinner of roasted chicken and potatoes for their guest. It gave her great satisfaction to entertain and have a purpose after the day-to-day dreariness of her life. Small talk continued throughout dinner for they were too polite to push the man for further news. After settling in the parlor, Meggie could hold her curiosity no longer.

"Rollie. Please tell us. Did you find your family? Did you find what you were looking for?" His responding grin gave her the answer.

"Oh, please tell us." She repeated eagerly.

Sonny leaned forward in his chair and chimed in. "We got all night, Rollie. Tell us what happened down there."

For the next several hours the Ryans lived Rollie's story. They laughed, gasped, grieved and marveled but never once lost interest as he shared the tales of a dozen lifetimes. Finally winding down, the three fell silent, savoring this special time, the peak in Rollie's world of valleys.

Suddenly Sonny jerked forward and snapped his fingers. "Just a minute! Just a minute here! Yes. Yes…..that has to be her."

"Has to be who, Sonny? What are you talking about?" Meggie asked.

"That Pettigrew woman he told about. The one whose husband was his father's best friend in the war…an they had that mule farm west of town. You know who I'm talking about Meggie. She's so old, she's covered in fossils. An mean…..that woman's as mean as a snake. Still raising an selling some mighty fine mules too. Or so they say," he chuckled.

Rollie could barely contain his excitement. "Miz Maribel Pettigrew! You sayin she's still alive?"

"Well, last I heard she was. Why don't we all take a ride out there after workouts in the morning and see if we can find her," Sonny suggested.

Late morning found the threesome standing in the barnyard of the Pettigrew place. A muscular, middle-aged workman emerged from the darkness of the open barn door, pushing a loaded wheelbarrow before him. He headed for the nearby manure pile with a passing glance in their direction and dumped the load. Shucking heavy leather gloves, he pulled a soiled handkerchief from a back pocket, wiped the sweat from his brow and walked toward them.

"You people lost or sumthin?" he asked insolently.

Rollie bristled at the man's manner but Sonny ignored it and greeted him politely.

"How do you do, sir?" My name is Sonny Ryan, owner of Ryan's Racing Stables out at the Fairgrounds. This is Mrs. Ryan and our friend, Mr. Burroughs. We're here to see Mrs. Pettigrew. Is she about today?"

"With a sweep of his eyes, he looked Sonny up and down, turned and flung, "I'll see," over his departing shoulder.

Sonny flicked his eyebrows at the other two and grinned with amusement.

"Huffy shit shoveler." Rollie snorted. "Wonder what his problem is….sides being ugly."

For the second time, the worker emerged from the darkness of the stable followed by a tiny bent figure. The old woman shuffled toward them, a cane clutched tightly in her hand. She wore an ankle length dust-covered skirt, black work boots, and a man's long sleeved plaid shirt, topped off with a black knitted shawl. Unruly silver streaked hair was pulled loosely to the nape of her neck and wound into a tight bun. Atop her head sat the dirtiest, ragged, rotten looking hat that any of them had ever seen. Filled with jagged tears, holes and stains, Rollie figured the only thing holding it together was just plain dirt. The woman's face was lined with age, her hands gnarled and arthritic, but the spark in her eye left no doubt that there was still a life left in her.

"How do, Mrs. Pettigrew," Sonny began. "My name is Sonny Ryan from…"

"I know who you are Mr. Ryan." She interrupted. But her eyes looked past him, past Meggie and fixated on Rollie's face. Catching her intent stare, he snatched his hat off and waited nervously with it clutched between his two hands. As she shuffled forward, Meggie and Sonny stepped back, mesmerized with her intensity.

"I know you," she almost whispered. "I know you boy." She stopped toe to toe with the man who towered over her. Through squinted eyes, she peered up at him and in another moment a slight knowing smile curled the corners of her wrinkled mouth.

"So. What did they decide to name you?" she asked coyly, having solved the mystery.

"Rollie, Ma'am. Rollie Burroughs." He replied with an emotion-choked voice.

"If'n I didn't know better, I would swear you was your Pa standing here in front of me," she told him. "I am so very honored that you came to see me."

After the visit with Maribel Pettigrew, Rollie thought his heart and his brain would surely burst from all the emotion. The concentration of recent month's input burdened him to tears shed in the privacy of his bed.

"Cryin like a baby," he cursed himself. Hon-ga gazed disinterested, his jaw working a tuft of sweet hay. "We gotta get out of here an back home ta where it's quiet, boy. My brain's about to bust with all this shit packed in ta it." With that he determined to leave on the first train he could find back to Idaho.

Looking for Sonny the next morning to share the decision, he found the little man walking one of the trotters in a back lot. The horse's front legs, covered with a black tar-like substance, were swelled grotesquely.   Gamely, the animal followed the man's lead, walking with an agonizingly, slow painful step.

"What the hell happened to him?" Rollie stopped short.

"Before, you say anything…. this isn't my horse." Sonny clarified. "He belongs to one of my borders. I'm just walking him…. has to be done couple times a day."

"What happened to him?" Rollie repeated, his eyes still on the horse's disfigured legs.

"It's called firing. Something new this guy heard about an wanted to try. Horse started to go lame from all the pounding on a hard track. Most people just sell them off when they can't race no more, but now they come up with this new thing. Theory is that if you put a new injury on top of an old injury…well, they're both supposed to heal in unison. Dammed ole wives tale if ya ask me."

"Injury?" Rollie's face began to redden with anger. "What kind of injury?"

"Little hot pokers….kinda like a big needle." Sonny replied glumly. "I won't do it to mine and after seeing this one, I don't think I'll be allowing it with my borders anymore either. They say you can get another year or two out of the horse after they over it, but I don't like it at all. I already told this guy; next time he can take it someplace else."

Watching the injured horse's stiff, painful attempt to walk convinced Rollie, his decision to leave for home was just. I need to git home and find the peace again, he reasoned.

Sonny helped Rollie load Hon-ga and Weaver into the livestock car. As before, he opted to ride in the back with them rather than the passenger car. He tied the animals, still laden with his belongings, to walk Sonny down the platform and bid him farewell.

"I reckon we won't ever see each other again, less un you an Meggie decide to come check out my neck o' the woods. I'd love to introduce you around ta all my friends out there."

"Well, good friend," Sonny looked kindly up into Rollie's face and took his hand. "I can't tell you what a delight it has been to Meggie and me both to know you and share a little of your life. I'm sure you won't be coming back and I'm afraid we're just a little old to be traveling that far to see you. But than again... you never know, do you? Be happy my friend. We won't forget you."

The words had barely passed Sonny's lips when the cracking sound of splintered wood, banging and the braying of a mule exploded across the loading dock. Dust blew from between the slats of the livestock car as it fairly rocked on the track. One more thump and then a man's hysterical yells, "Help! Help! Get me out of here!"

Rollie spun around and ran back to the livestock car, bursting into the darkened, dusky interior. A man cowered on the floor in the corner. The Palouse horse stood over him, while the enraged mule continued to bray and lunge with bared teeth. The man's shirt was torn and bloodied, his pants scuffed with dirt from the animal's hooves. While Rollie subdued the animals, two stockyard policemen came to the rescue of the injured man.

Rollie agonized that now he was in trouble and would never get out of the city. He patted and stroked the animals, calming them somewhat until a policeman reentered the car.

"What's your name and business mister?" he asked.

"Name's Rollie Burroughs an I was visiting here. I got passage on this train fer me an the two animals. We're tryin to git back home to Idaho. I don't want no trouble officer. Is that fella hurt bad?"

"Bad enough. They got him on a stretcher and taking him for the doc to check out. If he's okay the next stop'll be jail."

Rollie's eyebrows lifted in question.

"He's a railroad bum! A hobo! He was hiding in this car. When you went outside he was fixing to steal from your pack on top of that crazy mule there. He said the mule went loco an tried to kill im. When he went down the horse stood over im until you came runnin in." The man paused for a deep breath. "Look, just let me see your papers an then let's close this car up. Best thing you can do is get on out of town. We don't want to have to shoot your mule but it appears to me, he's a mite dangerous."

"Yes Sir." Rollie answered gratefully. After the man left, he pushed the sliding door shut with a bang and turned to the animals with a caressing hand and wide grin. "That's my good boys! My very good boys! Now let's git our asses back home where we belong."

22 *THE JOURNEY HOME*

Clickity clack, clickity clack. The clack noise accentuated with a jarring vibration as they traveled day after day. The first day out, Rollie found it irritating, the second day tolerable and after the third day it began to bear semblance to a rocking lullaby carrying him home. Weaver and Hon-ga traveled well as long as the supply of hay and a daily serving of oats held out. Their water buckets were filled at every refueling stop, as was their master's food supply. Lack of exercise would leave them stiff and tightly coiled but that would be cured in the first day or so after arrival.

The anticipation of returning home masked all the emotion and pain experienced in the preceding months. Finally alone in the livestock car with only the animals for company, he had much to ponder. Tension drained away with the staccato like sound of clacking wheels and rocking motion of the train.

I have done all I can do for now. It's out of my control an I jest have to wait fer home, he thought. It felt good to let it go.

A fresh bale of hay was opened, mounded into a deep nest and covered with a blanket. Safe in his nest, Rollie contemplated flicks of blinding sunlight that flashed between the car roof planks and why the wheels made the clickity clack noise. Going deeper, he thought about the life stories of his Missouri ancestors and where it had all come to. After all those people, a century of life stories and it ended with him and his baby sister, Emilie. Melancholy, he thought there was no one left after them and so it would end.

Before leaving the Ryans, Rollie explained with a certain amount of embarrassment that he could neither read nor write very well. "It's my own fault though, cause my old aunt did try. I wuz jest too stubborn to work at it. Meggie, would ya write a letter to Emilie fer me…please?"

"It would be my pleasure." She answered brightly.

What Rollie could have never realized that by asking her help, the favor was all his.

"Jest send it to Miz Emilie Coble in Antonia, Missouri. She'll git it okay. Tell her that I looked for Mr. Arley Hambeck an regret to inform her that he is passed away. If'n she gits to a time that she kin leave Antonia she knows where I'm at. Tell her that her big brother is waitin fer her."

He gave Meggie money for postage and slipped out to buy a bouquet of flowers that she would find after his departure.

A trace of a smile passed his lips when he thought of the Ryans. Sadness followed knowing that he would probably never see them again. Old Indian Billy, Doc Williams and Daisy the café owner completed the circle as he drifted off to sleep. Dreams of peace and hope filled the dark places where nightmares used to be.

Time passed quickly as he alternately slept, reconciled the past and planned for the future. He composed a little presentation for Cecelia Gideon and rehearsed it over and over in front of the animals. When he first spoke, they both pricked ears forward and watched him with interest. After the second or third presentation, Hon-ga went back to his sweet hay and Weaver simply looked amused. Rollie knew that was not so, for how could a dumb mule ever be amused? Irritated, with the animal, he turned to address the wall.

The speech began with a declaration of love, followed by the news of his small inheritance. He could offer her a home, either in town or on a small ranch of their own. He could finance a millinery business that would be hers alone. Whatever she wanted or could possibly need to be happy if she would only marry him. He would get down on his knees and beg if that's what it took. Cecelia was his future; she was the rest of his life.

On the last stop before their arrival home, Rollie laid out clean clothes from his pack and cleaned up in the water trough behind the station. Hon-ga and Weaver picked up his

133

excitement and began to stomp and knicker when the saddle and packs were cinched on.

As the train neared his own town, he peeked through the car slats and was greeted with the sight of the green and white wooden station building growing larger as they approached. The engine whistled to announce their arrival and hissed to a rolling stop with cars aligned to the rough wooden loading platform. Rollie pushed the heavy door open on squeaky, complaining rollers and smiled at the familiar sight of his town.

Freddy, the stationmaster, greeted disembarking passengers as he had for countless times before and directed them to the local cafés and facilities. When his attention finally turned to the livestock cars, he was greeted with the sight of a grinning cowboy leading his animals down the ramp.

"Rollie, Rollie," he rushed toward him with extended hand. "Dang! It's good to see ya again. Welcome home."

"Thanks Freddy. I cain't tell ya how good it is to be home. An what's more I ain't ever leaving here again," he declared.

"Oh wait up a minute," Freddy grabbed Rollie's sleeve as he turned to go. "I dang near forgot for a minute, I was so surprised to see ya. Miz Suzy Jane told me, if you showed up, to report down to the tavern right away. She's wantin to see ya. It's important."

"Important? Got any idea what it's about?"

"Naw, I'd rather not say. You just need to go see Miz Suzy Jane. That's all." Freddy turned and rushed back to his other passengers.

Hmmmph, Rollie snorted. Reckon I need something to eat first. She probably wants to warn me off Cecelia again and I'll need a full stomach fer that.

He led the animals to Strube's Mercantile, tied them to the rail outside and entered the familiar old store. The smell of good German fare and Mrs. Strube's pastries greeted him in the dim light.

"Ach, my friend Rollie," Mr. Strube called out in surprise.

Behind the counter, Mrs. Strube looked up and clapped her hands to her rosy cheeks. "Guten mornink," Herr Rollie, she greeted him cheerily. "Velcum hom!"

This is nice to have people happy to see me, the cowboy thought as he doffed his hat.

"Sind sie hungrig?" she asked.

Puzzled, Rollie did not respond. Mr. Strube shot his wife a dirty look. "Speak English. Speak English." Turning back to Rollie he explained. "She forgets vhen she is excited. She asks, are you hungrig?"

"Hungry! Oh, yes hungry. Ma'am I'm so hungry, my stomach thinks my throat's been cut."

Now it was the Strube's turn to be puzzled until they figured out the joke. With a chuckle Mrs. Strube said, "Ve have schwein endstücke un saurkraut and a very gud apple strudel."

Once again Rollie looked blank and turned to Mr. Strube for an explanation.

"Pig tails un saurkraut un apple strudel," he announced with delight.

"Umm, umm." Rollie faked pleasure with the menu. In dismay he tried in vain to avoid the experience of pigtails but could not do so without insulting the good couple. What the hell, he thought. I'm starving an one time ain't gonna hurt nothing.

Mrs. Stube heaped up a brimming plateful and he retreated with it to the back corner of the store. A wooden keg in the corner served as his dining table. With a fork, he delicately raked the skin back to find tender, juicy white meat on little bones. Simmered for hours in Mrs. Strube's homemade sauerkraut, it tasted wonderful. Looking up he found the couple watching for his reaction with some trepidation.

"Mrs. Strube, this here's the very best pigtails I ever et! Kin I please have a piece of that apple strudel now?"

After paying the bill, Rollie turned to leave when Mr. Strube called him back.

"Ach. I almost forgot to tell you. Miz Suzy Jane vants to see you. You go there mein friend."

135

Mr. Strube's face betrayed an emotion that Rollie could not interpret and a very bad feeling grabbed his gut. He nodded affirmation and started toward the tavern, leading his animals behind. Halfway up the street he met Sheriff Roy who gave him a warm greeting and welcome back home. Then the sheriff placed a hand on Rollie's shoulder and looked meaningfully into his face. Both tall men, not many people could stand high enough to look either one of them directly in the eye. With an unmistakable note Sheriff Roy repeated the message that already had been passed twice before.

"Yes Sir. Freddy an Mr. Strube have already told me. I'm on my way there now. There sumthin I should know before I git there?" he asked guardedly. "What's going on? Cecelia. Sumthin's happened to Cecelia!" he guessed.

"Miz Suzy Jane already knows you're back. She's waitin for you now." The sheriff said simply.

With pounding heart and a sick, growing sense of dread, he tied the animals and shambled up to the double swinging doors. Standing there in hesitation, the feeling of doom and sadness from old nightmares possessed him once again. Taking a deep breath, he pushed the doors open and peered into the dark haziness of the saloon. Nothing seemed out of the ordinary. To his left, Melvin tinkered on the old upright piano, two thirsty workers stood at the bar sipping beer and another followed a hostess up the back wooden stairs. His eyes scanned wooden tables throughout the center of the large smoke filled room and came to rest on Miz Suzy Jane who sat facing the door.

With a stern face she nodded acknowledgment of his presence and then with a pointed finger, indicated the chair setting opposite of her. As he reluctantly approached she called out to the bartender and waved her hand in the air. He immediately poured two shots of whisky, beer chasers and brought them to their table on a tray.

"This sumthin I'm gonna need?" he asked her somewhat sarcastically and lifted the shot glass in salute. Miz Suzy Jane sipped at her whisky and glared at him over the rim. Suddenly she slammed the glass down, splashing the amber liquid out on the scratched wooden tabletop.

"I told you to stay away from her! Didn't I tell you she was off limits?" She shrilled.

Puzzled he just looked at her for a moment. "What's yer problem woman? You don't own Cecelia. At least I reckon that's who ye're talking bout, ain't ya?" Without waiting for the answer he pushed on, his face beginning to redden with anger. "Just who the hell do ya think ya are telling people they cain't see each other if they want ta? I love that little girl. I asked her ta marry me afore I left an now, gawd dam it, I'm planning ta make it happen….an you kin jest go pound salt up yere ass fer all I care."

Rollie slammed down his glass, and stood up abruptly from his seat. Just as quickly, Miz Suzy Jane slumped over and began to sob.

"What the hell? " His mannered softened with the surprise of her response. "Sumthins not right here." Rollie declared simply as he sagged back down into the wooden chair.

The distraught woman looked up at him and in a quaking whisper said, "Cecelia is dead, Rollie. She died having your baby."

Chapter

23 *A NEW LIFE*

"That's bullshit!" Rollie pounded his fist down on the tabletop. Brimming beer mugs rebounded, sending the liquid splashing across the table surface and over the floor. Miz Suzy Jane looked at him with widened eyes, drawing back from his rage. Sheriff Roy who had been watching silently from the doorway walked across the room and eased into a chair within Rollie's sight. The meaning wasn't wasted on the enraged man but he could not let it go.

"Yere sittin there telling me that Cecelia's dead an it's my fault? I love her an I don't believe whut yere telling me. If'n she don't want me, she's gonna have to come out here an tell me to my face!"

"Rollie." Miz Suzy Jane clasped her hands together on the table in front of her place and stared down at them. "Cecelia Gideon is dead and she died having your baby. It's as simple as that."

She glared into his eyes with cold resolve and moments later he wilted under their hold. A knife had been plunged into the man's heart, hot tears burned his eyes and he shook his lowered head in disbelief.

"Sheriff Roy...is it true?" he looked up at the sheriff.

The sheriff nodded affirmation and leaned forward, his elbows rested on his knees.

"Miz Suzy Jane. I don't understand how it could be my baby. One day she said she loved me an the next time she'd say we wuz through. It was just once. Just the one time an it was a day that she loved me. I didn't mean it ta happen. It just did. She cried an said she wanted me forever an the next I saw her she said we wuz through. She kept turnin my head every which way. I jest cain't believe this."

138

"You dumb bastard, once is all it takes," she spate with renewed anger and rose from the table.

Moments later she returned with the tiny new baby wrapped tightly in a gray flannel blanket. Bending toward him she offered the bundle with extended arms. Hesitating, he looked up into her distraught face and then back down at the bundle. Reaching out with thumb and forefinger, he tentatively pulled a corner of the blanket down to reveal a round, pink face and velvet head. Pink, cupids bow lips moved in a sucking motion even though she slept.

"It's a girl." She said simply. "This is your daughter."

The saloon girls presented Rollie with a paper of rambling care instructions for the baby and the few meager supplies they had for her. None of it made sense to him so he climbed aboard the big horse, reached down for the grey blanketed bundle and then left them all without a backward glance.

The Palouse horse headed toward the Clyatt Ranch without any direction or urging from his master. He knew the way. The mule followed the lead willingly, the tiny bag of the baby's belongings added to his load. As they headed down the main street, town people glanced sideways at the sight while a few stopped and openly stared. Everyone knew the story of Cecelia and her baby. Had the father not returned there would have been no choice but to declare her an orphan and available for adoption.

Rollie ignored the nosy people, save for the Strubes, who received a curt nod as he passed their store. Mrs. Strube wiped away tears while her husband held her tightly to his side.

Shock, grief, embarrassment, fear…. the feelings churned within him. He clutched the tiny bundle with one arm and held the reins loosely with the other. These people look to me as though I was a killer, he thought with dismay. What am I going to do? I never even held a baby this little before. How kin I care fer her? Oh, gawd. Miz Sophie I need yere help now, he implored silently.

The Clyatt's young son, Shelby, assumed responsibility for Rollie's two other horses in his absence. Booger, the moonblind buckskin was easy as long as no one ever tried to ride him. But the newest addition, a wild black mustang that Rollie had wangled off of his Indian friend, Matthew, was something else again. At first, akin to a skittish wild hare, he bolted with every attempted touch. A breakthrough finally came on the day that Shelby simply ignored him and turned his affection, as well as a few oats, to Booger. Shelby's reward was a soft nose poke against the back, followed by a short session of snuffling. With each new day, the mustang got closer and closer until he could be petted, then groomed and finally halter broke to lead. Shelby came a long way with the wild horse and gloried in his accomplishment.

The longer that Rollie stayed away, the more concerned everyone became that he was even coming back. A question of the cowboy's well-being and even his very survival had recently come under consideration.

The day that Rollie and his entourage rode back into their lives was filled with happiness and relief. Miz Sophie was enamored with the infant and immediately took possession of her.

"Rollie, a couple of weeks after you first left here, Cecelia came by looking for you. I didn't think much of it at the time, but this sweet little baby here must be why." Sophie smiled down at the sleeping baby in her arms. "She seemed very upset when I told her you were gone."

"I just wish I'd aknown sooner Miz Sophie. I never would have left Cecelia. I jest cain't believe this. I don't know whut in the world I'm gonna do," he lamented. "To think, this on top of everything else that's happened."

"One day at a time Rollie," she cooed with her eyes focused on the baby. "We'll deal with it one day at a time."

The cowboy was hit still another time when Delmar Clyatt asked him to step aside for a little talk.

"I regret to tell you this Rollie, but when you were gone so long and we never heard from you, I could only assume that you weren't coming back at all. I had no choice but to give the foreman's job to someone else," he explained.

Rollie liked his job on the Clyatt Ranch and gloried in his status of foreman, so Mr. Clyatt's announcement came as another kick in the gut. He dropped his head and placed a hand over his eyes.

"When is this ever gonna end?" he asked no one in particular. "Who'd ya hire, fer the job, Mr. Clyatt? Do I know im?"

"I gave the job to Purdy Roxlo, Rollie….an he's done very well by me. Now that I've given him the job, I can't take it back. If you'd only stayed in touch I would have held the position for you."

"I know. I know, Mr. C. It's my own dam fault. If ya don't mind givin me a day or two to gather my senses, I'll jest be out of yere way here. I have to figure where to go and how I'm gonna take care of this baby. Shit! Mr. Clyatt. I don't know nuthin about taking care of a baby!"

"Simmer down, Rollie. Just simmer down." Mr. Clyatt soothed him. You don't have to go anywhere. If you're willing to stay on as a hand under Purdy, I'd be right lucky to have you. We'll work something out about the baby. In fact, it looks to me like Miz Sophie's already taken her over for now."

Day by monotonous day, Rollie worked at whatever needed to be done. Anyone but Purdy Roxlo would have given him a bad time and gloried in the role reversal. But Purdy remained a true friend and felt grateful for Rollie's presence. Rollie worked harder now than he ever had before.

Evenings and quiet days were spent learning to care for his daughter. Miz Sophie coached him on feeding, burping, bathing and diaper changes. But the dreaded "C" word, colic, scared him to death. Miz Sophie taught him to make a sugar tit out of a soft rag wrapped tightly around a lump of sugar. Dampened slightly she popped it into the baby's mouth to suck on. The next good trick Rollie learned by accident. After a hard workday, he was attempting to placate the screaming baby and put on a clean shirt at the same time. Flustered, he finally gave up with the buttons, lifted the baby and cuddled her against his warm bare chest. In a very short time, she stopped crying and fell asleep, with a tiny thumb in her mouth. When he discussed the incident with Miz Sophie they rationalized it was the warmth from his body that eased her colic.

As Rollie's confidence with the baby grew, he fashioned a body sling that crossed over his chest and around his neck. He rode about the ranch on Hon-ga, the baby asleep in the sling. As they rode about, he sang and talked to the child, much to the amusement of the extended ranch family. Who would have ever imagined Rollie Burroughs, tough man, at the mercy of a little pink baby?

After a lot of thought and prodding from Miz Sophie, Rollie finally decided on a name for his daughter. The memory of his little grand-mére singing French lullabies and baking sweet treats for him was one of the few that made him happy. How could I ever go wrong by calling this precious child Marguerite, for her great grandmother, he pondered?

When pressed for a name for the black mustang by Shelby, that came easily as well.

"His name is Red River the second," he declared with no hesitation. An if he turns out to be half the horse as the first one was…. well, he'll be a pretty dam good horse."

As Marguerite grew and became more active, Rollie found it increasingly difficult to spend time with her and give the job his best effort. To Delmar's increasing annoyance, Rollie's work performance began to drop off.

The favorite spot after the baby's naptime was on the front porch of the bunkhouse. The cowboy leaned back in one of the wooden spindle chairs, his feet braced against the porch railing. Little Marguerite, sat on his lap facing him, her back resting against his elevated legs. She clutched his thumbs in tight little fists and grinned up at his big face as he discussed all of life's mysteries with her. She giggled at his antics, blew bubbles and squealed to her father's delight. Rollie Burroughs was hopelessly in love with his precious infant daughter.

"Marguerite, I never knew it was possible to feel so much in my heart for another living thing. Yere the greatest gift

I ever had in this world an, little girl, I promise to do my very best for ya, whatever it takes."

Junior Pelley, unbeknownst to Rollie, leaned against the bunkhouse doorframe watching and listening.

"That's a mighty cute little baby," he remarked in his prissy manner. "Too bad about her Ma though."

Rollie looked around, slightly embarrassed to have been overheard.

"Yeah," he answered simply, hoping that Junior would take the hint and go away.

Junior was the son of retired missionaries. Most of his fellow cowboys on the Clyatt Ranch disliked him because of his self righteous, hypocritical ways. A little man, he always looked spotlessly clean, even after a full day of work. Church in town every Sunday morning was a must and he openly criticized those who did not share his devotion and austere ways.

Junior continued to stand in the doorway, gazing at the baby. Rollie sensed he had something else on his mind and started to feel irritation with the intrusion.

"You want sumthin Junior….cause if ya don't, I'm kind of havin a private talk with my daughter here." He held Marguerite's little hands and smiled into her face while talking to Junior.

"Well, I was just thinking how hard it's going to be for her when she's old enough to know…an folks treatin her different an all."

Rollie's back stiffened and a subtle throbbing started in his temples. He wasn't sure what Junior was referring to, but knowing him so well, he knew it was probably something malevolent…like his nature.

"Jest spit it out Junior. I ain't got time or patience fer games," Rollie suggested with a casualness that he did not feel.

"It's just you an her ma not being married an all, folks won't be so kindly towards her. Course no one on the ranch feels that way," he added hastily, "but I was just thinking about when she finally has to leave here and go places."

The throbbing in Rollie's temples turned into a crushing pain, and his face flushed a hot red. He closed his eyes and tried to breath slowly. Had the little girl not been on his lap, Junior Pelley might have died that day, or at least wished that he had. As Rollie struggled to keep control, he looked down at Marguerite's face. So sweet, so trusting, she smiled at him. He could not help but to smile back at her.

"Junior, it seems pretty plain to me that the only person either here or in the town to even bring it up is you." Rollie twisted around in his chair to look Junior in the eye. "Now whut does that say about you?"

Junior flushed, turned around and quickly disappeared into the bunkhouse.

That night Rollie lay awake in his bunk staring at the black ceiling. Whut am I doin here, he thought. I got the means to be independent an on my own but I'm still hangin on here. Miz Sophie's been good to help me with Marguerite but she's got her own work too. I cain't keep takin advantage even when she tells me she loves it. The Clyatt's are good folks but there's no future fer me here. I need to figure sumethin with a future. Sumthin to give to my girl one day. I want to teach her whut really matters, whut's really important in life an not jest pleasures like Purdy does, an mean spirited like Junior. Now Matthew's mom 'n dad, Mary 'n Two Feathers, they knew what ta teach him growing up. He knows whut counts. That's how I need to raise my girl.

A surge of pleasure passed over him at the thought of the Nez Perce family. Sumthin to think about. How kin I make that kind of life fer my little girl? He draped an arm over his face and tried to sleep.

Another week passed with Rollie becoming more disheartened with his present life. When yer not sure whut ta do, don't do anything, he repeated the old adage silently in his head. Hot and tired he stepped up on the bunkhouse porch and walked toward the door. Thinking he heard a disturbance in the corral he paused for a moment to look back. Then turning back toward the building again he heard Junior Pelley speaking to an unknown audience within the darkened room. Hearing his

144

name mentioned, Rollie moved quietly toward the doorway and stood behind the mean-mouthed little man.

"I been praying on it every night an talked with the preacher but it still comes down to the same thing. Those two had sinful relations…and their baby was born out of wedlock." He leaned toward the other cowboys who now stared past him at the hulking man in the doorway. In a lowered conspiratorial voice, Junior hissed, "And you know what that makes her!" Then straightening up, he closed his eyes, pointed a finger skyward and declared loudly, "In the eyes of the Lord, they are all born in sin and going to hell!" Junior opened his eyes and looked to his audience for approval only to find them looking beyond him with horrified faces. Slowly he turned and at the first glimpse of the furious man behind him, shrieked and covered his face. "Oh God, oh God save me," he wailed, rocking to and fro. The cowboys backed away, trapped with no other available exit, save the door.

Shelby Clyatt and Purdy Roxlo also heading to the bunkhouse had stopped behind Rollie on the porch. They, too, heard Junior's moralizing discourse. Shelby quickly placed a hand on the big man's rigid shoulder and talked in even tones and clipped sentences.

"Rollie. Rollie, listen to me. Rollie, he ain't worth it. You got a daughter to think of now. Back away now. You're a better man than he'll ever be. Rollie, back away and come with me…..now."

Somehow the young man's tone and demeanor penetrated the red heat that enveloped his head. He began taking rapid shallow breaths and his body softened under the pressure of Shelby's hand upon his shoulder. Then, two deep ragged breaths and Rollie focused his eyes on the pale, quaking man before him.

"Junior Pelley. You look me in the eye cause I got sumthin I want to say to ya right here, right now in front of everyone."

Junior looked up at Rollie between trembling fingers that still covered his face.

145

"I weren't raised up the way you wuz Junior an I thank God that I wasn't. What little training I did git, I know enough ta not judge other folks, I know to not gossip an bad mouth im, and I know that I could never hurt others the way that ya do. I'm a better man than you Junior Pelley. Every man here is better than you. Not long ago, I probably would have killed ya for what I jest heard out of yer mouth. But I'm a different person now. I'm a better person, an because I am better, I'm gonna let ya go on this one. Jest don't ever git yer ass in my way again or it ain't gonna be a good day fer neither of us."

Rollie turned to leave, then paused for one last shot.

"Ever Sunday you practically break the church doors down ta git inside. I used to laugh bout that Junior. But ya know what? I'm glad bout it now, cause church is where sumbody like you needs to be."

Junior fell to his knees sobbing in embarrassment and relief when Rollie finally walked away.

24 *THE GOOD LIFE*

The morning after Rollie's confrontation with Junior Pelley, he asked Mr. Clyatt for time off, packed his clothes, put Marguerite in the sling across his chest and rode toward the mountains. Three days later he was back, but without Marguerite.

The Rollie Burroughs who came back from the mountain was a different person. Excitement for life sparked from his eyes and his step was light with the pure joy of living. Dusk approached as he rode into the Clyatt's yard and he went directly to their house. Removing his hat, he knocked at the door. When Miz Sophie saw him standing on her front porch, she broke into a broad grin.

"Rollie, it's so good to see you," she said with relief. Then looking at his empty arms she asked, "But where's Marguerite?"

"Miz Sophie, please don't be upset, but I left her behind with Mary and Two Feathers. I've come back to talk with you and Mr. Clyatt...please."

"Yes, yes of course," she said hesitantly and backed aside so he could enter the house. "Delmar, Rollie is here to see you," she called.

"I'm wantin to talk with you too, Ma'am," he corrected her.

Sophie ushered him into her warm kitchen, where Delmar finished the last of a bowl of dried beans, ham and cornbread. Without even asking she dished up a deep bowl of the steaming beans with trimmings for Rollie, poured coffee all around and then sat at the table with the two men. After wolfing down his satisfying meal, Rollie pushed back and gave the patient couple a loving smile.

"I got sumthin to tell ya an it ain't gonna be easy fer me. I, ah…I'm gonna be leaving the ranch Mr. Clyatt."

"Just a minute, Rollie." Delmar interrupted. "If it's Junior Pelley you're uncomfortable with, the matter has been resolved."

"What?" Rollie reacted.

"After that incident the other day, the men all got together and told Purdy they didn't want to work with Junior anymore. Purdy told him to pack his things and leave. You see, Rollie, you have a lot of friends here."

The big man lowered his head sadly.

"Much as I despise what Junior said, I still don't hate im. Mr. and Mrs. Clyatt, I've learned so much about life an people, an even about myself of late, that Junior Pelley jest ain't important at all. He's jest sumbody to feel sorry fer. An I do regret that he had to leave on my account though. I wouldn't have wanted that."

"It wasn't on your account, Rollie." Sophie reached across the table and placed her hand over his. "It was on his own account. He should be half so wise as you. We were so very proud of how you handled yourself out there with him."

Rollie flushed at the compliment.

"Thank you Miz Sophie. Um… I jest feel so bad to tell ya though. I'm still gonna be leavin here. Ya see, most my life has been wasted in a sense, cause I had no cause, no purpose to give my life a meaning. I jest passed through every day until now. I got this precious, little new life dependin on me ta do the right things an I found a place to really give myself to."

Delmar tipped his head quizzically.

"I'm partnerin up with Matthew, Mr. Clyatt. We're gonna breed the best Palouse horses ya ever saw, an sum day I promise yere gonna be hearing bout em an hearin bout us."

The couple's eyes widened with the shocking announcement and Rollie rushed on before they could react further.

"Ya see, Matthew's at a place where he's got the land, an he's got the base herd, but he needs horses with new blood, corrals an barns, pastures. Folk's are startin to look im up.

148

There's a market out there fer the horses he's raisin. Two Feathers is too old to help much anymore an that's what I do best. I bought half share of the business with my family's money. Not the land," he emphasized, "that belongs to the Indians...jest the business part. Marguerite's got a whole family up there to love her an to raise her up right. The Indian school's nearby an she's gonna be goin there with little Daniel when they're both old enough. My only sorrow is leavin all of ya an this place. Ya been good to me an I ain't ever gonna ferget it."

"But Rollie, you and Marguerite will be coming back to see us won't you?" Sophie pleaded.

"Yes, Ma'am. You kin count on us, cause I don't want Marguerite to ever fergit ya either. I'll always be obliged fer how ya helped me with her, Miz Sophie. I couldn't have made it without ya." Rollie's eyes misted with deep emotion. "Oh, un Miz Sophie, there's one more favor I'd ask of ya an then I promise ta not impose anymore. Would ya please write a letter fer me?"

Sophie smiled sweetly and nodded.

"I told ya bout my sister, Emilie Yeager. Write her at Antonia, Missouri an tell her whut happened here since I been back. Tell her there's a life for her here if'n she wants it. Would ya tell her all that fer me Miz Sophie?"

By the time they finished coffee and jawing around the kitchen table, the rest of the ranch was asleep. Rollie put Honga in a stall with feed and hay and then slipped into his bunk. He lay awake for a good while listening to the chorus of snoring, grunts, mumbling and groans from his fellow workers. I think I'm actually gonna miss some of this, he thought before finally falling asleep.

Rollie rose before sunrise with the other cowboys and enjoyed his last breakfast with them. An ancient black cast iron stove graced the bunkhouse and was put to good use every day by an equally ancient, half crippled cowboy, nicknamed Cookie. Cookie's one and only job in life was to cook two square meals a day for the hands and to clean up afterward. The rest of his time was spent sleeping and whittling on the front porch. Cookie was a very contented man.

After everyone left on their various jobs for the day, Purdy stayed behind for one last talk with his old friend.

"Rollie, old buddy, I missed you so much when you were gone such a long spell, but somehow I knew you'd be back and I had that to look forward to. But this time is different. You're not comin back and I'm feeling mighty low about it."

"Well, the same holds fer me too Purdy, but I will be comin fer visits from time ta time….an it's not like ya don't know where to find me. The road runs two ways, ya know."

They both stared at the floor for a few minutes until Purdy jerked back sharply.

"But for the life of me, I just don't see you and Matthew….Matthew, of all the people in this world, for you to partner up with! I could see you and me, or you and most anybody else, but you two don't even like each other! There was a couple of times over the years that I thought one of you would kill the other… and you spent half your waking hours either picking at him or thinking of mean things to do to him. And if that's not enough to wonder about, I can't begin to guess why he would even want you."

Rollie grinned and nodded his head in agreement.

"Purdy, we talked bout all that an we both agreed. It ain't been the same fer neither of us without the other. It's the pepper in our life, it's what makes us do better, an go harder. Kin ya understand that? I wuz so dam jealous of that little rat faced runt fer so long, cause he had the good things in life that I wuz missin. He had love, a family, a history, an a purpose to life with those Palouse horses. I got all that now too, an in a way I have him to thank fer pushing me to find it. Sure, we're probably gonna butt heads almost every day of our lives but I really do like him…an together we're gonna make sumthin special up on that mountain. You'll see Purdy. Jest be happy fer me okay?"

Purdy pursed his lips and nodded in agreement.

"Oh, un one last thing," Rollie added in afterthought. "Don't ever tell anybody, especially Matthew, that I said I like im. Best to keep im a little skittish all the time." He raised his eyebrows in question.

"I won't." Purdy laughed and raised a hand in farewell.

Shelby Clyatt's early years in the east were happy. He resented leaving his grandparent's comfortable home to join his parents in this primitive new life they chose for the family. For the first few weeks he pouted in his room and avoided the ranch activities. That attitude took a quick turn about after meeting up with Rollie, Matthew and Purdy. Under their tutelage he became an avid horseman, naturalist and could cuss with the best when his parents were out of hearing range. Matthew extended Shelby's new world even further with an introduction to the Nez Perce culture through his parents, Mary and Two Feathers. Shelby loved the Indian family and spent many happy days visiting with them. Matthew even gave a fine spotted horse to the boy.

In the last year, Shelby had shot up in height equal to Rollie's own. His frame was thin but a deepened voice and shadowing on his lip and chin confirmed approaching manhood. When his parents informed him of Rollie's decision to leave the ranch he was devastated. One by one, his mentors were leaving, he was growing up and the inevitable changes could not be prevented.

Rollie found Shelby in the darkened barn. His little mustang, Red River, was tethered to a post where Shelby curried and brushed the sleek black hide.

"Shelby, I cain't thank ya enough fer all the care ya gave my animals whilst I wuz away. Ya did a good job gentling ole Red River here. Turns out ya have a real gift with horses."

The boy continued brushing and did not look up nor acknowledge Rollie's comments. When Rollie tried to approach the boy, he turned away to hide his tears.

"Shelby. I know my leavin hurts ya. But look at it this way…I'm still nearby. You kin still come up to see us like ya always did before an we'll be comin back here too. Nuthins changed, cept the distance tween our houses. Besides all that, look at how yere growing up. Your Pa an Purdy will be needin ya to help out on the ranch more an before ya know it, yere gonna be runnin this place. With all that, ya need to stay strong."

Shelby sniffed loudly and turned to face Rollie.

"I know. I know." He said sadly. But I guess I won't be here much longer myself, Rollie. They're sending me back east for college. Guess I'll be staying with my grandma and grandpa for a few years again."

"College!" Rollie was stunned. "Boy, ya grew up on me an I never even noticed. Gosh, I'm right happy fer ya Shelby. An whut will ya study? Whut do ya want to be?"

"There's not a doubt in my mind Rollie. I'm going to be a writer." He answered enthusiastically.

"Is that right....an whut will ya write about?" Rollie pressed.

"Everywhere I look, there's a story. I've already started to write about my adopted Nez Perce family. I plan lots of visits to see all of you up on that mountain. I just know there's another great story coming with you and Matthew partnering up to raise Palouse horses. Should be a lot of laughs along the way too." He added.

While Rollie saddled Hon-ga, Shelby strapped the cowboy's belongings on Weaver, the mule. Red River and Booger, the moonblind buckskin, were tethered behind Weaver. With only one short backward glance and a wave of his hand, Rollie rode out the gate and down the dusty road with his little caravan. Shelby stood by the gate and cried as he watched them leave.

THE END

NOTES FROM THE AUTHOR

Rollie Burrough's story is more than a work of fiction. His character is actually a combination of several people that I have known. He is a sensitive, good-hearted person with a passion and respect for what is decent in life. In addition to his own shortcomings, he struggles with a low tolerance level for people who practice disrespect, dishonesty and cruelty to others.

As previously mentioned in the Acknowledgements, some of the incidents and much of the background for Rollie's Story were inspired from my own Missouri family history. They were modified to fit the storyline and characters. For example my Grandfather, William Shuttleworth, actually raced his Standardbred trotter, Dr. Friel, at the 1904 World's Fair in St. Louis. I still have the second and third place ribbons that they won there. Paul Burroughs's black mustang, Red River, was modeled after my own mustang who was originally named Red River. He is now called Smokey Joe. Ole Doc Williams's buggy seat dog, Rowdy, was also real. I will leave the rest to the reader to decide what is real and what is not. As with my first book, The Palouse Horse, I sincerely hope that you enjoy reading this sequel as much as I have enjoyed researching and writing it.

I find it sad to think that the sacrifices of those who came before us, as well as so many momentous events of the past are either completely unknown or casually discarded in today's busy world. It is my wish that Rollie's story as well as Matthew's will inspire us to learn more of our own history and appreciate the things that are really important in life.

BIBLIOGRAPHY
& ACKNOWLEDGEMENTS

Author unknown: *A Summary History of German Freethought in Missouri:* freethought.mbdojo.com

Author unknown: *Alton In The Civil War:* www.altonweb.com

Borein, Edward. Etcher and Illustrator

Ethier, Eric. *Civil War Times Magazine*

Goodspeed's History of Missouri

Goodwin, David. *The St. Louis Arsenal*

Kirschten, Ernest. *Catfish and Crystal*

Missouri Historical Review: The State Historical Society of Missouri, Columbia
> *Les Indiens Osages:* French Publicity For The Traveling Osage. (Translation)
> Edited by Margot Ford McMillen

Rule, G.E. *Blair & Lyon, Save the Union*

Time-Life Books. *The American Indians*